Murdered by Human Wolves

The Werewolf Saga Apocrypha
Book 1

Steven E. Wedel

MoonHowler Press

MoonHowler Press
Oklahoma, USA

Cover art by Kirk Alberts

DEDICATION

Murdered by Human Wolves is dedicated to Alex, who went with Dad in search of a grave marker despite some misgivings about the existence of werewolves. You're a good kid.

The above dedication was written in 2004. My oldest son was a boy of 12 at the time. He's 22 now, a man living away from home and taking care of himself. However, I'll always remember the day we drove down to Konawa and I teased him about the biker behind us being a werewolf chasing us away from the cemetery.

ALSO BY STEVEN E. WEDEL

Darkscapes

Little Graveyard on the Prairie

Seven Days in Benevolence

After Obsession (with Carrie Jones)

Unholy Womb and Other Halloween Tales

Amara's Prayer

THE WEREWOLF SAGA

Call to the Hunt

Murdered by Human Wolves

Shara

Nadia's Children

AS EDITOR

Tails of the Pack

Preface to the Final Edition

The temptation here is to write a scathing denouncement of the small press publishing world. It was less than eighteen months ago that I expressed hope that a new publisher would prove to be a redeemer, a light in the dark of the horror genre's independent publishing scene.

But that was not to be.

Graveside Tales Publishing released an edition of this novella in October 2012, with the rest of The Werewolf Saga books to follow, divided up into a series of novellas, a plan I never did like. But after the publication of this first volume, the train derailed and Graveside Tales went on hiatus.

It's a new world in publishing, though, and so I took control of the series and released *Shara* and *Ulrik* myself, along with the never-before-published new novel *Nadia's Children* under my own MoonHowler Press imprint.

Unlike other publishers I've dealt with, Dale Murphy proved to be a good guy. He stayed in communication and, in lieu of whatever money his edition of *Murdered by Human Wolves* earned, he signed over the rights to the original cover art by Russell Dickerson. I'm very proud to be reusing Russell's cover on this MoonHowler Press reprint.

The interior content of this edition – with the exception of this Preface – is identical to that put out by Graveside Tales in 2012.

But that's enough from me. The werewolves are waiting, and they are not patient. Thank you, reader, once again, for choosing to give my story a read. You are much appreciated.

—Steven E. Wedel
Moore, Okla.
February 2, 2014

Introduction
by
W.D. Gagliani

What is it about werewolves? Why are so many of us drawn to the wolf rather than the bat?

Besides the doubtlessly harmful ubiquitousness of "all things vampire," there may be legitimate reasons the werewolf is making a literary comeback of sorts.

Perhaps it's our fascination with the Beast Inside—the dark alter ego we all harbor. The werewolf is a perfect metaphor, reminding us that we all share a capacity for monstrous behavior, whether we acknowledge it or not. Perhaps it's the tragedy of random victimization—either the monster's or its victim's. The werewolf is usually portrayed as a most unwilling monster, trapped in its tragic destiny. Somehow the werewolf's blood-and-guts post-Change hangover strikes a deeper chord than the coolness of a black-clad, shades-wearing vamp out on the town for a spot of vintage O-neg. Perhaps it's the lure of the animal itself—the wish-fulfillment of wanting to be free to romp in the woods and let our wild side out for a while. And, of course, there's the moon's influence—perhaps we werewolf lovers stare up into the night sky at the mysterious orb with longing, sensing its pull on our emotions. Or sanity.

Whatever the case, the werewolf fascinates us as it has fascinated—and frightened—many through the centuries. Whether due to undiscovered mental illness, an unknown disease such as porphyria, or some other sort of rational affliction, you have to take it seriously when hundreds of people throughout the world were tried and executed for lycanthropy...

Steve Wedel is one of us. When he looks up at the moon, he thinks wolf thoughts.

With *Murdered by Human Wolves*, Wedel has perpetrated the best kind of speculation. He has taken some facts and a mystery, and shaped a construct around them that will make you wonder, as in all the best monster tales, who are the true monsters. For that is often the lesson of our history of intolerance, that those we label "monster" are more likely to be victims of our own petty fears, jealousies, and hatred. We know Katherine Ann Cross lived a short seventeen years into the 20th Century, and her grave marker reads: *Murdered by human wolves*. But we don't know what that means, exactly. Steve Wedel has filled in what he thinks might have happened to young Katherine, and it makes for a riveting beginning to his *Werewolf Saga*.

Let Steven Wedel tell you a story, a mysterious and tragic story based in fact. Then let yourself heed the moon's call.

Keep Howlin',

—W.D. Gagliani
Oak Creek, WI
October 2007

Foreword

Katherine Ann Cross did exist. She was born in 1899 and died in 1917. Very little is known about her, though it is generally believed she died because of an illegal abortion. Her grave marker in the cemetery near Konawa, Oklahoma, states that she was "Murdered by human wolves."

It is said that there were many such epitaphs on grave markers in this cemetery and others in the region from that same time period, though many have been defaced, stolen, or are simply no longer legible. Some people say they have seen ghostly shapes and heard unattributed growling or howling sounds near the grave of Katherine Cross.

I have incorporated into this piece of fiction some newspaper accounts, local legends, and information obtained through interviews of people familiar with the history and location of the grave. However, this tale is *not* meant to be an historical record of the life and death of Katherine Cross. Nor is it an indictment or exoneration of any other actual people mentioned herein; Elise Stone, Dr. A.H. Yates, and the schoolteacher, Fred O'Neal all were actual citizens of Konawa. Luther and Thomas McGrath, as well as many other minor characters, are people of my own invention. This is simply a story, one that builds on fact, legend, and speculation in a way that incorporates it into my own fictional world of The Werewolf Saga.

The interview contained in the feature article that follows this story is real. It was conducted with paranormal investigator Mary Franklin, done over several e-mail messages and one face-to-face discussion. I have not embellished on her tale in any way; what she had to say was strange enough.

Do I believe it? I'm not going to bias you one way or another with my beliefs. Read it and decide for yourself.

I will say this: By all accounts, Katherine Cross died an unnecessary and likely very painful death at a young age.
Rest in peace, Katherine.

—Steven E. Wedel
July 6, 2003
Moore, OK

Murdered By Human Wolves
Based on a True Story
Steven E. Wedel
KATHERINE
dau of
JT & MK
CROSS
Mar 13, 1899
Oct 10, 1917
Murdered by human wolves
CROSS

Katherine

"You did what?" Katherine Cross asked.

"I did it," Elise Stone repeated. "I gave myself to Luther McGrath. I ain't no virgin no more."

"Why'd you do that?"

"'Cause I wanted to. He says it ain't no big thing. He says men and dogs don't have no inhibitions about sex and women shouldn't neither."

"Inhi-what?"

"Yeah. You know, thinking it's all dirty and bad. It's a natural thing, he says."

"My daddy says he's the devil, or working with the devil," Katherine said. "And Mama said I better stay away from him."

"He ain't no devil. He's just a man," Elise said, laughing. "I saw him naked and he ain't got no tail or no horns or nothing."

"Nothing?" Katherine giggled.

"Oh, he's got *that*."

"How ... how was it?" Katherine asked. "Did it hurt?"

"Hurt sumpin fierce at first," Elise said. "But then, I don't know, it felt purty good. I liked it. He said there at the end I was moving like a woman with experience."

"Elise! No!"

"That's what he said."

Katherine snickered into her hand, her eyes straying across the dusty street to the lumber mill where her father worked. She kept walking without saying anything until they were past the mill and almost out of the little town of Konawa, Oklahoma. "My daddy'd skin me alive if he knew I was talking to you about that kind of stuff," she said. "He'd call you a ... a whore, Elise. Lots of folks would if they knew."

"I ain't no whore," Elise said. "I just done what's natural, like a horse or chicken or dog would. Like Luther said."

"We ain't animals, Elise. People are supposed to get married before they do that."

"That ain't what Luther said. He said marriage was just sumpin people made up to pretend we're civilized."

"Don't you want to be civilized?"

"Not especially. It was fun. The second time we did it, he was growlin' and I swear I was screamin' like a demon from Hell 'cause it felt so good."

"The *second* time? You mean you done it with him more than once?"

"'Course I did. We been meetin' down to the creek regular, just 'bout every evening."

"Aren't you worried you'll get pregnant?"

"If'n I do, I reckon we'll just have to get married real quick so's people won't know."

"They'll know, Elise. Old Mrs. Collins'll count the days from your wedding until when the baby's born and she'll go straight to the newspaper."

"Let her. I won't even care. I got to go, Katherine. Mama wants this flour to make biscuits for supper."

"Okay, Elise. I'll see you later." Katherine stood quietly as Elise started up the lane that would lead her home. "Elise," she called. When her friend turned around, Katherine said, "You be careful."

Elise only laughed and skipped away, the basket holding the supplies she'd bought at the general store bouncing heavily at her hip. Katherine continued west, then turned south at the cemetery, following the county road that divided Seminole and Pottawattamie counties, until she came to stand at the gate of her own home.

She was eighteen years old and had been born in the home she shared with her parents. As she opened the gate and walked up the path to her front door, she studied their little home, made with lumber John Cross had milled, and wondered what it would be like to live in one of the big cities she'd heard about, maybe Kansas City or Denver or even New York City.

Two of her father's three coonhounds raised their heads to look at Katherine as she came up the three steps to the porch of the house. The third only raised an eyebrow as he opened an eye, then closed it and resumed his late summer nap. The other two hounds lowered their heads. One, the female Katherine had named Bonnie, thumped her tail a couple of times, as if to say she wouldn't be opposed to the human's attention, but it really didn't matter.

"Not now, girl," Katherine said. She pulled the screen door open and went inside to the smell of beef cooking in the great iron stove her father had bought from a store in Oklahoma City two years ago. Katherine remembered how proud her mother had been to have that hulking blue and silver stove squatting in her kitchen, having been forced to do most of her cooking over a fire in the hearth for so many years.

"That you, Katherine?" Mary Cross called from the kitchen.

"Yes, Mama." Katherine went to the kitchen and plopped her sack of corn meal onto the table.

"Thank you, dear. Did you have a nice walk?"

"Yes. I met Elise in town and we walked home together."

"How is Elise?"

"She's fine."

"And her family?"

"They're all fine," Katherine said, watching her mother measure out the grainy yellow powder from the bag. "Mama, why does Daddy say Luther McGrath is the devil?"

Mary stopped, her measuring cup poised over a bowl.

She looked up at Katherine, her brow crinkled and the little lines around her eyes suddenly seemed very deep to her young daughter. "You stay away from that man. And his family, or friends, or whatever they are."

"I will, Mama," Katherine promised. "But what's wrong with them?"

"You ever see Luther McGrath in church?"

"Well, no, but maybe he's a Presbyterian."

"That man's no Presbyterian. He's no Christian. You mark my words on that."

"That makes him the devil?"

"That makes him somebody you stay clear of."

"I will, Mama," Katherine said. "Has he done something bad?"

Mary pursed her lips, then sighed before answering. She dumped her corn meal into her bowl, then cracked an egg and let the yolk run over the meal. "Not that anybody can prove," she said.

"What do folks think he's done?"

"Unspeakable things. Nasty things. Murder. And worse."

"What's worse than murder?"

"Things you don't need to trouble yourself with. Why are you asking about Luther McGrath?"

"No reason." Katherine dropped her gaze.

"Katherine Cross, you tell me or I'll tell your father you've been asking."

"It's not me, Mama," Katherine said. "It's Elise. She's ... I guess he's courting her."

"That man is after Elise?" Mary's voice was filled with panic. Her weathered hand went to her chest, then she fanned her face. "Elise Stone?"

Katherine knew she'd said too much and tried to think of a way to take it back. "I don't think it's really courting, Mama," she said. "Elise was just saying he'd talked to her and she thinks he's a handsome man."

"The devil wouldn't take an ugly shape," her mother said.

"If folks think he's killed people, why ain't he in jail?"

"Nobody can prove he did it. Lots of us just think he did."

"Who's he supposed to have killed?"

"Girls mostly." Mary stopped stirring milk into her cornbread mix and looked Katherine in the eye. "Girls about your age. Mostly in Thackerville."

"How long's he lived in Konawa?"

"Since the town was moved after the flood," Mary said. "Folks thought they was moving away from trouble when they moved after the flood. All of a sudden, though, Luther McGrath and his kin were neighbors."

"He came in the land run, like you and Daddy?"

"Yes."

"He's lived here all that time and nobody's proved he killed anybody?"

"Katherine, I've heard enough about Luther McGrath for one day. For one lifetime. You stay away from him. You understand me? Him and all his kin."

"I told you, Mama, I'll stay away."

All during supper, Katherine worried that her mother would mention her questions about Luther McGrath. Katherine didn't want to have to face her father's questions about why she was asking. She'd never been able to lie to her father and she didn't want to worry him over a problem that really only concerned Elise's father. As she ate, she stole glances at her mother, waiting to see if she'd bring it up, but she seemed to ignore Katherine, paying attention only to her husband's account of his day on the job.

After supper, Katherine helped with the dishes, then went outside to help John with the evening milking. They kept about a dozen milk cows, along with the team of two mares that pulled the wagon and the plow, several chickens, a few geese and the hounds.

"What did you do today?" John asked as he brought the first of the milk cows into the barn. Katherine helped guide the cow to the feed trough, then placed the sliding boards against her neck, just behind her head, so she couldn't pull away from the food and disrupt the milking process. She sat on her stool as John brought in another cow to milk.

"Nothing much," she said. "Did my chores this morning, then went to town for Mama to get some corn meal."

"I saw you and Elise walk past the mill this afternoon. You two girls sure seemed to be talking about something serious."

"Oh, it was nothing," Katherine said, glad there was a cow between her and her father. "She's sweet on somebody."

"Oh yeah? Who would that be?"

Katherine bit her lip and wished she hadn't added that last sentence. "I can't tell you that, Daddy," she said. "Elise made me promise not to tell." That was the truth. Katherine pulled two teats and watched the milk squirt into her tin bucket. The cow shifted and swished her tail. Katherine continued rhythmically pulling and squirting.

"It ain't Luther McGrath, is it?"

Katherine's hands froze on the cow for a moment, then she recovered. "Why would you think that?"

"There's been talk in town. Some secrets can't be kept."

"Daddy, I really can't say. I promised."

"You're a good girl, Katherine. You got to keep your word. But you know we, your mama and me, we don't want you having anything to do with McGrath and his folk."

"I know that, Daddy."

"Stay clear of them."

"I will."

"All right. You got that cow milked yet?"

"Yes."

"Then let's get these girls out of here and bring in a couple more."

The July evenings were still very hot. After the milking, Katherine and John joined Mary on the front porch of their house. Mary was mending torn clothes. John idly strummed a guitar. Katherine sat quietly, flipping through a Sears and Roebuck catalogue she'd nearly worn out.

"Find anything you like in there?" Mary asked.

"Lots," Katherine answered.

"Like what?"

"This dress, for one thing." Katherine held the catalogue up so her parents could see the pink dress with the long, billowing skirt and ribbon at the bosom. "I'd wear it to every dance."

"And you'd be the prettiest girl there," Mary said.

John grunted. "She's already that," he said.

They sat quietly for a while. When the sun sank below a hill and the sky was stained orange and pink on a gray backdrop, Katherine excused herself and went inside. She fell asleep listening to her father strum an old love song as Mary murmured the words.

Katherine

Morning came early, as it always did. Katherine was in the milking barn before the sun came up and had shuffled five cows through the line before John finished feeding the horses and joined her.

"Your mama's fixing bacon, biscuits and gravy," he said as he led in his first cow. "I could smell it in the stable. We ought to be done here just about the time she takes the biscuits out of the oven."

They worked quickly, squeezing the milk into tin pails, dumping it into large cans and sealing the cans. The milk from the evening milkings was for the family, stored in a large wooden icebox in the root cellar behind the house. The morning milk was taken into town and sold to a dairy store before Katherine's father went to his job.

"There's not enough," Katherine said, studying a half-empty can and counting cows in her head.

"How many did you do before I got here?"

"Five."

"You're right. We're missing one." Together, they went to the back door of the barn. The cows, relieved of their swollen utters, were roaming deeper into the pasture, eating the tall grass that was drying in the hot summer sun. "Nobody waiting," Katherine's father said.

"That's not good."

"Nope."

"Think somebody stole her?"

"Could be. More likely, she's stuck in mud down by the creek or got out of the fence. I don't have time to find her this morning."

"I'll do it, Daddy," Katherine volunteered, knowing

he expected her to do it. "I'll go right after breakfast and find her."

"All right. If you can't get her, if she's stuck or something, come into town and get me."

"Okay." They went inside, washed up and sat down to a hot breakfast of thick bacon and fluffy biscuits swimming in cream gravy. After breakfast, as John was loading the cans of milk onto the wagon, Katherine tied on a sunbonnet and set out to find the missing cow.

"Watch out for coyotes," John called after her. Katherine waved back at him, ducked between two strands of barbed wire fence and headed for the tree line to the west of the house.

The sun was up. The morning was still young, but already it was brutally hot and humid. The long, dried prairie grass bent under the hem of Katherine's skirt, then popped upright to tickle the insides of her calves as she walked through the field. By the time she crossed the hundred yards to the trees, she was thankful for the shade they provided. The belt of trees nearest the house was about forty feet thick, divided by a creek. Katherine entered the trees and stopped on the bank of the creek. She looked down into the shallow red-brown water, looked right and left, but didn't see the missing cow.

There'd been one there once before, she remembered. It had taken her father and four other men to pull the cow out. Like now, the weather had been hot and the creek shallow. The cow had simply stood too long in the water and sunk past her knees. As she struggled to get out, she sank deeper, which caused her to fight harder. Some of the men had to put ropes around her horns and pull while two others pushed her from behind. One of the men behind had been kicked hard in the shin, leaving a huge knot. Katherine's father took the man to see Dr. Yates in town and paid the bill himself. The cow hadn't given any milk for about a week after that incident.

But there was no cow stuck in the creek today. Not at this spot, anyway. Katherine followed the creek north to their property line, then turned back and headed south. John Cross owned three hundred-sixty acres of land. He'd claimed one hundred-eighty in the land run, then bought out a neighbor who decided farming wasn't all he'd hoped. The woods thickened the further south she went. The creek widened and became swampy as it neared the South Canadian River. Frogs croaked in the rising heat of the day. A myriad of bird sounds filled the air and mosquitoes swarmed around Katherine. She swatted at the bugs and watched for the snakes that lived nearer the river. She didn't like any snakes, but the water snakes absolutely terrified her.

She decided the trees were too thick and no cow could have been walking through them. She backtracked to where the creek was narrower, took off her shoes, hiked up her skirt and waded across. As she slid a shoe back on, she glanced up at the sky and saw the buzzards. Four or five of them were circling low not far to the west. Katherine tied her shoelaces and climbed up the low bank of the creek. More prairie grass stretched before her, waving just a little on the gentle swells of land. A few hundred yards west of the creek, two buzzards jumped into the air as one of the circling birds disappeared into the tall grass. Katherine started toward the spot.

To her left were more trees, growing along the bank of the river. To her right was open prairie. A couple of miles ahead, beyond her father's property line, were more trees where another creek joined the river. Between those trees and herself were the feasting buzzards. Katherine knew that many birds could only be feeding on something as large as a cow. But, she had to see for herself. John would question her to be sure it was their cow and not a deer or wild pig.

As she got closer, she could hear the harsh calls of the buzzards and see their bald, pinkish heads bobbing above the grass line. Some, having gotten their fill, ran a few yards and launched their ungainly bodies into the air, but more replaced them. So far, the carrions didn't seem bothered by the approaching girl. Katherine couldn't yet see what it was they were devouring.

"You don't really want to get any closer, lass."

Katherine jumped and let out a small shriek. Blood thundered in her head and she felt her heart thudding quickly and heavily in her chest. She looked in the direction of the voice and at first didn't see anything, but then a man detached himself from the shadows of the trees and stepped into the late morning sunlight.

"It's a dead cow they're eating," the man said. He was bare-chested and barefoot, wearing nothing but a tight pair of buckskin trousers. A tall man, at least six inches taller than Katherine's father, with broad shoulders and thick arms, he stopped while still several feet from the girl. He crossed his arms over his very hairy chest and looked at her, a smile playing over his lips. He wore a moustache that was as thick and black as the hair that framed his face. The moustache covered his upper lip and reached down the sides of his chin like two sharp stakes. A thin streak of beard grew below his lower lip, disappearing at the bottom of his chin.

"Who are you?" Katherine asked.

"Thomas, they call me. Thomas McGrath, at your service, m'lady." The man gave a deep mock bow. As he did, Katherine noted an odd scar on his left shoulder, something that looked like an X with a triangular cap on it.

McGrath! He's a McGrath. What's he doing here? What do I do? Katherine looked behind her; home seemed such a long way away.

"You're trespassing, Mr. McGrath," she said. "This is

my daddy's land."

"Ah, is it now? Well, I didn't realize that. I was down by the river, you see, when I noticed the buzzards flapping around. I thought I would come have a look. To make sure no one was hurt and getting themselves eaten up by the birds."

"You say it's a cow?"

"Yes, lassie, a cow. A fat one. Holstein, I believe you call that breed. White with the big black spots."

"How ... Do you know how she died?"

"Wolves got it, I'd guess. I wager the buzzards surely didn't do all the damage to a beast that big and healthy."

"Wolves?"

"Yes'm. Surely you've heard the wolves calling at nights."

"I guess," Katherine said. "I thought it was just coyotes."

"Oh, no ma'am," Thomas said, uncrossing his arms and taking a few steps toward Katherine. She crossed her own arms and stepped back. The man stopped and smiled, then hooked his thumbs in the waist of his pants. "Coyotes, they have a high-pitched yip. But your wolves, the big timber wolves especially, have a deep howl. A beautiful howl. The opera of the night, it is."

"You seem awful fond of killers," Katherine said.

"They do what is in their nature," Thomas answered. "I respect them for that."

"You sound just like –" Katherine stopped and bit her lower lip.

"Like who?"

"Nobody."

"Your friend Elise?"

"More like your friend, the one she talks about. Luther McGrath."

"She is sweet on him," Thomas said, smiling broadly so that his goatee didn't look so harsh. "And he on her, if

I do say."

"It ain't right, what they've been doing."

"And what is that they've been doing?"

"You know what, I think," Katherine said.

"Tell me." His tone dared her.

"S–sex," Katherine said. "They've made love. She told me so."

"Ah, that they have. I've seen it, myself, with these two eyes."

"You *watched* them?"

"It's not like they were hiding it."

"They should. It should be in the bedroom. Between a woman and her husband."

"They had the sky as their roof, the moon as their bedside lamp and the dewy grass as their mattress. All created by God himself," Thomas countered. "Would you say a room created by man is more fitting?"

"Well ..."

"The morning has worn away, my lady. I suspect you'll be wanting some lunch."

"I should get home, now that I know what's become of the cow."

"'Tis a long walk. Would you have lunch with me? I have plenty in a bag beside the river."

"I–I shouldn't," Katherine said.

"I mean you no harm," Thomas said. "It's only dried beef and bread, but it's here and you don't have to walk all the way home for it."

"Really, thank you, but I couldn't."

"You're a wise girl, Katherine Cross," Thomas said. "A wise girl not to go into the woods with a stranger you've only just met."

"How did you know my name?"

"Ah, lassie, I've seen you around town. And Elise has talked about you a great deal, as well."

"She has? She talks to you? I mean ..."

"You think she just raises her petticoat for my cousin and runs away without speaking to his family?"

Katherine could feel the hot blood rushing to her face. She turned away from the man and started walking home as quickly as she could without running. She heard him laughing behind her, then suddenly he was beside her, his hand gently but firmly taking hold of her elbow and stopping her.

"I did not mean to offend you," he said. "I forget that not everyone shares our views on the natural working of nature. There is no shame in what your friend does, nor in what my cousin does. It is natural. Didn't God say to go forth and multiply?"

"Is she ... She'll get pregnant."

"That she will."

"She'll be disgraced. People will call her names. They'll ..."

"Throw stones at her? Drive her out of their town? Hang her? I have seen all those things done, and more."

"Why? Why do you and your cousin and kin do this? Why did he bring Elise into this?"

"She was not a hard one to convince," Thomas said. "But maybe you could talk her into mending her ways."

"I tried that yesterday."

"She will be meeting with Luther again tonight. Maybe if you were there and interrupted them she would see the shame you think she should feel for what she is doing." He arched his eyebrows as he spoke and Katherine realized for the first time that he really had only one long, bushy brow that spread over both eyes and the bridge of his thin nose.

"Do you really think it would help?"

"I think if anyone can change her mind, it is her friend Katherine who she talks about so much," Thomas said.

Katherine thought about it for a moment, calculating

whether she could sneak out of her parents' house, whether she dared. *It's for Elise. To save Elise.* "Where do they meet?"

Fred

"Just look at them, the devils."

"Let me see." Fred O'Neal held out a hand for the binoculars, but they were not immediately turned over to him. "Let me see, Doc."

Dr. A.H. Yates handed over the binoculars. Fred put them to his face and peered through the branches of the shrub where he was hiding with the doctor, looking down the hill toward the creek. Figures that had been indistinguishable because of the distance were suddenly identifiable. "There he is," Fred said. "There's Luther."

"The lead devil, himself," Yates agreed.

"I wonder what they're talking about."

"Devilry. Murder. And worse."

"Worse?"

"Better dead than to become what they are."

"What about Elise?" Fred asked, spying Elise Stone among the group of about twelve other figures, mostly men. Some were gathering wood to build the bonfire they made each night they gathered at the edge of the McGrath land. Others were laying out food or already drinking from whiskey bottles. Elise Stone hovered near the clan's patriarch, Luther McGrath, her eyes fixed on his face, a smile never leaving her lips. If the man was still for more than a moment, she reached out to hold his arm, touch his shoulder or run a finger through the long jet-black hair that hung down his back.

"What are we going to do about them?" Fred asked.

"Some will have to be killed," the doctor answered.

"The others? Elise? Is it too late for her?"

"I've not seen one of them bite her. I worry more about her womb."

"You mean ... ?"

"It's a feeling I have. A prophecy I've heard, told to me by a professor who came to America from Berlin. They are looking for one that can be created naturally, without violence."

"Without violence?"

"Yes. But when that one comes ... Then there will be violence enough for all the world."

"And you think they're trying to create that one with Elise Stone?"

"I think she is one of many."

"Many?" Fred lowered the binoculars and looked at the older man. Dr. Yates flicked his gaze toward the schoolteacher, then looked back down the hill.

"Many," the doctor said. "I have already treated some."

"What do you mean, 'treated some'?"

"The congestive chill that has claimed some of my patients lately. It has been the chill of my scalpel that killed them."

"You mean—"

"Yes. I mean I killed them when I learned they had been there." He pointed down the hill to the growing revelry. "Some, boys and young men mostly, came to me looking for treatment for the bites. The bite makes the victim very sick. I gave them the only treatment that would cure them. The one that would keep the number of werewolves from growing in this town."

"How many?"

"Several."

"We should do something," Fred said. "We should notify the police. Maybe go up and talk to the sheriff."

"They'd believe you, wouldn't they?"

Fred was quiet. Down the hill and across the creek, the bonfire was roaring. Faintly, Fred heard fiddle music and whooping. The night was growing dark. Silhouetted figures danced between the fire and where the schoolteacher and the doctor hid several hundred yards away.

"It's getting too dark to see them," Fred said. "Should we move closer?"

"Not if you value your life," the doctor said. "They have the hearing and sense of smell of a dog or better. If they found us, or even suspected we know what they are, they would tear us apart."

Already there had been too many bodies found slashed to ribbons and partially devoured around the area. Until he'd gone to the doctor asking about the illness claiming the lives of some of his students, Fred had believed the reports that the dead were victims of the Ku Klux Klan. He thought they had been found and dined upon by coyotes before the remains were found by another human.

"Who's that?" The doctor pointed past Fred to a figure walking down the hill in the direction of the fire. The schoolteacher raised the binoculars and looked through the gathering gloom.

"My God," Fred said. "I'm almost sure that's Katherine Cross. It is. It *is* her. What's she doing here?"

"Another lamb seduced by the wolves, no doubt," the doctor said.

"We've never seen her here before."

"No, but with her friend, the Stone girl, already down there, it was only a matter of time."

"We should stop her. Warn her what they are."

"It's too late. If we approach her now, we could be seen with her. That would be fatal to us."

"We can't just let her go down there."

"There's nothing else we *can* do. We should leave. The party is getting loud and some of them may go prowling soon."

"But Doctor ..."

"Is she worth your life, Mr. O'Neal? She isn't worth mine. If you go, you could be connected to me. I won't let you put me in danger." From his crouching position, the doctor opened his jacket to reveal a revolver tucked into his belt. "It is loaded with silver bullets. For *them*." He jerked his head toward the fire below. "But they would work just as well on an uninfected person."

"You would shoot me? For trying to save her from them?"

"If it means protecting myself."

Fred looked back toward Katherine, who now was nearing the brush at the bottom of the hill, where the creek cut through the land. She was far too close to the revelers now. "Dear God, look out for her," Fred whispered.

"Let's go," Dr. Yates said. "Quickly but quietly, like always. Stay low until we're over the crest of the hill." The doctor eased away from the shrub, remained hunched over, and scurried toward the top of the hill. Fred watched the doctor go over the top and disappear. He looked back down the hill. Katherine was hesitating, hiding behind a clump of brush, watching the activity across the creek.

Fred was about to risk slinking down the hill toward Katherine, to whisper to her from hiding that she should run, when a figure broke away from the shadows at the bottom of the hill and approached the girl. Katherine jumped, then seemed to relax. The two figures faced one another and appeared to talk.

Good God! How long has he been on this side of the creek? Are there others ...

Fred turned and hurried up the hill after Dr. Yates.

Katherine

"My dad would kill me if he knew I was out here," Katherine said. Thomas McGrath had startled her when he suddenly appeared beside her. She'd been hesitating, knowing that if she crossed the creek there'd be no getting away from the people gathered around the large fire without being seen.

"For trying to save your friend, he'd kill you?" Thomas asked. His smile seemed very bright in the moonlight.

"For sneaking out of the house," Katherine said. "And for talking to ... A lot of people don't like you and your family."

"Including your father?"

"Maybe."

"Shall we cross the creek? I should tell you that Elise has been making gestures toward Luther all evening. It won't be long before he gives her what she's wanting."

"Is it that bad?" Katherine asked. "Is she so bad that she's actually asking for ... for it?"

Thomas laughed. "You still say it as though she were copulating with Satan himself. Have you never had a boy touch you?"

"Never!" Katherine said. "I wouldn't."

"Do you say that because you know it's wrong, or because you've been told by your mother, your father and your minister that it is wrong?" Thomas asked, the smile still tugging at his lips, making the glossy black goatee twitch like a living thing.

"Maybe they say it's wrong because it is."

"And maybe it's because that's what they were told. There was a time, when the world was younger, that men and women loved one another freely, without being bound to one mate."

"That's heathen talk," Katherine said. "It was before people were civilized."

"It was before they were Christianized, you mean," Thomas said. "A patriarchal religion has to keep a tight fist around the sensual experiences."

Katherine struggled to reply but could think of nothing to say. "Take me to Elise," she said at last. "Let me get her and get away before my father realizes I'm gone."

"Shall I carry you across the creek?"

"I can walk. It's not deep." Katherine pulled her skirt up to her knees, ignoring the widening smile of Thomas McGrath as she exposed her ankles and calves. She hadn't worn shoes; they would have made too much noise crossing the floor of her house. She stepped into the cool water of the creek, felt her feet sink into the soft mud, and hurried across. As she stepped onto the bank of the other side, Thomas landed beside her. Katherine let out a screech and lost her balance. She fell into the creek, clawed in the mud for a moment, and emerged from the water gasping and spitting. Thomas was laughing at her again.

"Are you okay, lassie?" he asked.

Katherine looked from one creek bank to the other. It had taken her more than a dozen steps to wade through the water. She lifted a hand dripping with mud from the water and pushed a wet lock of hair out of her face. "Did you really jump all the way across there?" she asked.

"Of course I did," he answered. "Is that what frightened you?"

"I've never seen a man jump that far before," she said.

"Then watch this," Thomas said. Without a running start, he crouched, then sprang forward, clearing the water again and landing on the other side. "Now, watch this," he said, backing away a few paces. He rushed at the creek and launched himself into the air.

Katherine watched, awed, as the dark-haired man turned a complete somersault in the air over the water and landed on his feet on the other side. When he turned to look at her, an expression of satisfaction on his own face, she became aware that her mouth was hanging open. She closed it. "That was very impressive," she said.

"Thank you." Thomas stepped toward her, a hand extended. Katherine took the hand and let him pull her to her feet. Her dress clung to her and she was very conscious of the way it exposed the curves of her body and the shape of her legs. She wiped a hand across her rear and it came away covered in more mud.

"There's no way I'll be able to clean this and have it dried before Mama sees it," she said.

"I think we can help you," Thomas said. "Come with me."

He led her up the bank and into the light of the roaring fire. Several people, over a dozen, looked at them as they approached. Many called out to Thomas, raising a bottle in salute. Most of the people were of the McGrath clan, Katherine noted, but not all. She saw a few faces of people she recognized from town, some were boys and girls she had gone to school with. Most looked away when she met their gaze.

"Katherine!" Elise flew from the shadows and wrapped her arms around Katherine, hugging her and turning her in circles. "What're you doin' here? You're all wet. Was that you we heard fall in the creek?"

"It was me," Katherine said. "I'm here because of you. I want to take you home."

"Home? But, I don't want to go home," Elise said. "And besides ..." She paused and looked around. "I was savin' this, but I already told Luther. I might as well tell it to everyone now."

"What?" Katherine asked. "What is it?"

Elise turned around, holding Katherine's hand in one of her own, waving over her head with the other. "Let me have your attention," she yelled. Slowly, the crowd quieted, all eyes turned toward the two women. "Ya'll have become like another family to me," Elise said. "And now, I reckon we'll be family for real. Luther made me pregnant. I'm gonna have his baby."

The McGraths erupted in cheers. Some of the others cheered, as well, but Katherine dully noted that not all of her fellow townspeople thought the illegitimate pregnancy was good news. She pulled Elise toward her.

"You're pregnant?" she asked. "Are you sure? Do you know what this means?"

"It means I'm gonna have a baby," Elise said. "I'm gonna get married."

"There's really no need for a marriage."

Katherine looked away from Elise to see who had spoken. Luther McGrath stepped forward and put a hand on Elise's shoulder. Katherine fought the urge to back away from the tall, lithe man. He had eyes like black holes under a single eyebrow that was much darker and thicker than his cousin's. He was clean-shaven, and kept his pitch-black hair long and loose around his shoulders. Luther smiled at Katherine, showing a set of teeth that seemed mostly too small, except for the canines; it looked like he had filed those slightly. Katherine pulled her gaze from Luther's face and looked at his hand for a moment before finding Elise's face. She had to look back at Luther's hand, unsure what she had seen was right. The back of Luther's hand was covered in short, curled black hairs and his fingers all seemed to be almost the same length.

"What'd you mean, no marriage?" Elise asked.

"My people do not believe in your marriage ceremony," Luther answered. "I've claimed you as my mate. No one else would dare touch you while you are carrying my son."

"It could be a girl," Elise said. "And my daddy'll come down here with a shotgun and make you marry me now."

Luther smiled again, but it was a slightly menacing smile. "I can deal with your father."

"Luther, Miss Cross fell into the creek and got her clothes wet." Katherine had almost forgotten about Thomas, but now he was beside her, talking to his cousin about her.

"Yes. That is a shame," Luther said, nodding. He turned his attention back to Elise. "Why don't you and Katherine go to the creek. You can help her wash herself and her dress, then we'll put it near the fire so it will dry quickly."

"Okay, Luther," Elise answered.

"But ... What will I wear?" Katherine asked.

"I think we have a robe you can wear," Luther said. "You go ahead and I'll send it with Elise."

"I'll stay with you until she comes to help," Thomas offered. He motioned for Katherine to follow him, and she did.

"This is not going at all like I planned it," Katherine said as they walked back to the creek. Standing close to the fire had made the mud on her hands start to dry and harden. She closed her hand into a fist and the dirt crumbled.

"Things seldom do go as planned," Thomas said. "I think you'll find a bit of privacy over here." He pointed to a slight bend in the creek where the brush was thicker. "If you want privacy, that is."

"I do. Thank you," Katherine said. She followed the man into the brush, where he turned to face her.

"You seem considerably nervous, lassie. There's no reason to be."

"My best friend just announced she's pregnant and she's not married. I came to save her from that happening and it's too late. Now here I am about to take off my clothes with a bunch of people I don't know just not very far away but I have to do it so my mama and daddy won't know I snuck out of the house. I think I have reason to be nervous."

Thomas smiled again, his teeth flashing in the moonlight. "After you wash, I can give you a drink of something that will ease your mind."

"I don't drink whiskey. My daddy won't allow it."

"Your daddy's not here," Thomas reminded. "But it's of no consequence. I wasn't talking about whiskey. This is a warm drink from our home country in Europe. It will relax you."

"I don't know—"

"There you are." Elise crashed through the brush and stopped before Katherine and Thomas. "You don't have that dress off yet? I got the robe. Come on. I have to help you before I can go back to the party."

Katherine looked quickly at Thomas. "I guess I should wash."

"Yes. You should," he agreed.

When he made no move to leave, Katherine said, "Please go so I can undress." Laughing, Thomas turned and slipped away.

"Hurry up," Elise said, tossing the robe aside and pulling at Katherine's dress.

Reluctantly, Katherine stripped off her clothes and stepped into the creek. She quickly rubbed the mud from her body with fresh water and stepped back on the bank. Elise scrubbed mud from Katherine's dress, and motioned with her head to where she'd dropped the robe.

"I'm 'bout done," Elise said.

Katherine picked up the robe. It was heavy and made of animal hide. In the light of the moon and stars, the fur appeared to be gray. The hair was short and soft. "What is this?" she asked.

"Coyote, I think," Elise said without turning back. "Or wolf. I don't know. I wore it the first night I was here, too. Luther spilled whiskey on me. I couldn't go home smellin' like a still. I washed my dress right here, too."

"You mean, you had to take off your clothes your first time here, too?"

"Yep. Kinda funny, ain't it?"

"I guess," Katherine said. She slipped into the heavy robe, which seemed to swallow her into a warm pocket of stale human sweat and an animal musk. "This stinks," she said. "And it's so hot."

"It's just for a while. Your dress'll dry purty quick by the fire," Elise said. "There. I think that's all of it. Let's go." She wrung the water from Katherine's dress, hung it over an arm and pulled her friend through the brush and back toward the fire.

"Elise." Katherine stopped walking and grabbed the other girl by the arm. "I came here to take you home. Thomas said if I came here and confronted you that maybe you'd realize this is all wrong. He said—"

"Thomas said that?" Elise asked. "He's a liar. He's just sweet on you is all. He told me he's been wantin' ta get to know you."

Katherine stood still, looking at Elise, trying to find words, but not knowing what to say. *He tricked me.* Elise broke away and went to the fire, where she spread Katherine's dress on the ground near the flame before retreating to the shadows where her lover waited. Katherine pulled the front of the robe tightly closed and remained where she was. A few moments later, Thomas McGrath was at her side, a cup of liquid in his hands.

"You tricked me," Katherine said. "You knew Elise wouldn't leave here because of me. You just wanted me to come here. Do you know how much trouble I'd get in just for being here? And ... and to be naked?"

"You're not naked, I can tell you that," Thomas said.

"Under this robe I am."

"And I'm naked under my own buckskins."

"You know what I mean. And this robe stinks. Who would make a robe of coyote skins, anyway?"

"Those aren't coyote skins. It's wolf. It's a magic robe."

"Magic?"

"Sure. Luther brought it all the way from the Old Country."

"What's it supposed to do?"

"It gives you the power of the wolf, of course," Thomas said.

"Wolves are killers. They should all be killed. We'd be better off without them," Katherine said.

"You don't know the wolf, lassie. Here, I brought you that drink I promised." He held the cup toward Katherine. She caught the scent of peppermint coming from the pale liquid.

"What's in it?"

"An old family recipe for calming the nerves. It was my grandmother's. It's just water and herbs. I added some peppermint just for you."

"Aren't you drinking any?"

"I'm a whiskey man, myself. But, if you think maybe I'm trying to poison you ..." He lifted the cup to his lips and took a swallow, then wiped his goatee and offered the cup to Katherine again. She took it, but didn't drink yet.

"Thank you," she said.

"Aye. We'll be dancing soon, round the fire. You're welcome to join us if you're of a mind."

"I doubt it," Katherine said. "Not without my clothes."

Not saying anything more, Thomas turned away and went to join a small group of men. Katherine sniffed at the drink. It smelled very nice, minty and soothing. The cup was warm in her hands, but not hot. She raised it to her lips and took a tiny sip. The fluid was thick, like orange juice, but smooth and sweet. Katherine swallowed, then took a longer drink.

Somebody began to play a drum. As if it was a signal that could not be resisted, everyone moved toward the fire and began to circle it. Katherine watched as the circle moved faster and the dancers gradually became more animated, jumping and throwing their arms around their heads. She saw Thomas and noted that he'd removed his shirt again, revealing the strange mark he bore on his left shoulder. The muscles of his back rippled as he danced, stirring an unknown emotion deep in Katherine's breast.

Elise danced round and Katherine saw that her friend had opened her blouse. The buttons appeared to be gone, as if Elise had torn the garment open. The blouse gaped, revealing Elise's firm breasts and taut nipples as she twirled and skipped round the fire.

Katherine sipped her drink again. She felt lighter, somehow, as if all her cares had ridden a rope from her belly up her chest and right out of her head. When a boy she'd gone to school with appeared dancing round the fire, his own shirt discarded to show his pale, hairless chest as his arms flailed around him, Katherine smiled and had to cover her mouth to keep from laughing.

After another drink, Katherine realized she'd been tricked again, that the drink she was enjoying so much was some sort of drug. *Maybe he just mixed it too strong. Thomas doesn't seem so bad.* Katherine felt her eyes crossing and forced them to focus again. This time she did laugh, at herself, because she almost fell forward. She tried to stand still, but found herself swaying with the beat of the drum.

The next time she saw Thomas, he was naked. In fact, most of the dancers were naked. Katherine gaped at the sight of his flaccid penis bouncing in his lap as he leapt into the air and shook his fists at his sides before spinning out of sight again.

Some dancers were pausing at one point in the circle to have symbols painted on their bodies by a very old woman with long, thick gray hair. Many of the dancers also had that symbol branded onto their shoulders. The old woman seemed to feel Katherine looking at her and turned her own gaze back toward Katherine.

Her eyes are glowing like lanterns.

It somehow didn't seem strange to Katherine. She thought to herself that glowing eyes would help the woman see to paint in the dark. The sight of the naked dancers, including Elise, no longer seemed so out of place, either.

"You may as well join the dance." Luther had come to stand beside her. "You already are moving with the drum."

Katherine tried to speak, but her mouth felt gummy and slow. Finally, she found her voice. "I couldn't. I can't dance in this heavy robe, anyway."

"Let me help you." Without waiting for protest, Luther took the shoulders of the robe, slid it off Katherine's arms and let it fall to the ground at her feet. "You are wonderful. It is no wonder my cousin is so taken with you. Why don't you go and join him."

Katherine looked from the fire to the man at her side. He seemed so large and solid, like an oak tree or mountain come to life. He still wore his dark clothes. His eyes and hair were like glossy chunks of coal as he looked at her. He motioned toward the fire again. "You want to join them."

Katherine nodded. Luther took her by the hand and led her to the fire, placing her in the ring of dancers behind Thomas. "Dance," he said. Katherine had to move or be trampled by those behind her. At first, she only walked, but the drum beat from somewhere in the shadows, telling her she had to move faster, had to put her heart into the dance. She lifted her arms above her head and tentatively hopped into the air. She turned in a circle, dropped her arms, lifted her face to the night sky and jumped forward.

At one point, she felt sure she saw a piece of her dress laying at the edge of the fire, one fragment of skirt that had not burned when the garment was thrown onto the flames. She wasn't sure, but she had a feeling she had been the one to kick the dress into the fire.

Sweat formed on her body as she danced, sliding down her flesh, stinging her eyes, making her skin glisten in the firelight. Those around her also had a bright sheen of perspiration reflecting the orange light from their skin. Katherine found herself staring more and more intently at Thomas as he danced before her, noting how his muscles moved, how graceful he was and how his own eyes lingered on her nakedness.

Finally, Thomas stopped and pulled Katherine from the circle. They stood before the ancient woman with her jar of paint. Thomas held Katherine by the forearms, both of them panting from exertion. "Is she going to paint me?" Katherine asked.

Without answering, the crone reached up and swathed thick, warm paint across Katherine's cheeks. Then she ran a thick line from Katherine's throat, between her breasts to just above the dark hair of her crotch. All the while, the woman never spoke. Katherine remembered thinking the woman's eyes had glowed, but they weren't glowing now. Thomas released her and stood up straight as the woman painted similar marking on his body. Katherine watched, envying the woman for the way she was handling the lean, muscular man. Without realizing she was doing it, Katherine reached over and put both her hands around Thomas's bicep. It was firm and thick. He looked at her and smiled.

"Go," the old woman croaked at them when she'd drawn a line from Thomas's throat to his own private area.

"Come with me," Thomas said, taking Katherine by the forearms again and urging her forward. Katherine allowed him to lead her a short distance from the fire. He stopped and pulled her close to him. There was a moment's hesitation when she knew he was going to kiss her, and then his mouth was over hers, his arms crushing her against him.

Katherine didn't fight it, although deep inside she felt a nagging sensation that what she was doing wasn't right. Her arms circled Thomas as if they had become serpents with minds of their own. Her hands sank into his thick hair, slid down his neck and gripped his strong shoulders. When he pushed his tongue into her mouth, Katherine felt a shock of something hot and sharp and good rush through her body. She raised onto her toes to push her face closer to his. Thomas's hands explored freely over body, gliding softly over her buttocks before pausing and squeezing gently, then firmly before moving slowly up her sides to cup her breasts. When his fingers found her nipples and gently squeezed them, it felt so good that Katherine broke the long kiss.

Thomas attacked her throat, kissing and sucking, one of his hands moving to her hair and clutching it so he could tilt her head away from his, allowing more of her throat to be revealed to his hungry kisses. His tongue licked the sweat from her neck and shoulders, sliding down, down to her breast, where he suddenly sucked greedily. Katherine gasped and wrapped both her arms around his head, pulling him tightly against her. When she released him and he rose again to his full height, she felt his stiffened member prodding her belly.

She'd never seen one before. Katherine looked down at Thomas, amazed that the organ she'd seen hanging limply in his lap at the start of the dance was now much bigger, thicker, standing away from him, pointing to her as if she was the chosen one. Keeping one hand on his shoulder, Katherine reached between them with the other and gently gripped his manhood. A soft moan came from his throat and he smiled at her.

"It's so big," she said.

"Let me show you." Thomas put his arms around her again and lifted her off her feet. He laid her in the grass and placed hot, demanding kisses on her face, throat and breasts before opening her legs and positioning himself between them.

"Will it hurt?" Katherine asked.

Without answering, he took himself in his hand and guided his spike of flesh forward until it pushed against her. The sensation was forbidden, frightening, but Katherine wanted it to happen. She nodded, giving permission. Thomas leaned forward, pushing himself into her.

The pain was intense. Katherine groaned, arched her back and clawed at the dry grass as Thomas's shaft, which seemed even more massive as it pushed into her, slid deeper and deeper into her body. Then it stopped. She could feel his groin pressed against hers. She kept her eyes closed, scared of what would come next. He backed out, but not all the way. Just when she felt sure he was taking the thing out of her, but before she could decide if she wanted him to remove it, he came forward again, slowly plowing through her flesh and spilled blood until he was pressed against her once more. He pulled backed again, then pushed forward, his rhythm increasing.

Katherine opened her eyes, her head still thrown back. The first thing she saw was painted men and women, still dancing, but it was wrong. She squinted at them for a moment before realizing they were no longer dancing around the fire. They were dancing around her, celebrating the loss of her virginity with whoops and howls and cheers and ... *howls!*

Katherine looked again. Not all the shapes were human. Some of them were something else, still on two legs, still dancing, covered in hair, with deformed hands and feet and ... and the heads of wolves. She opened her mouth to scream. That's when she saw the beast on top of her.

Instead of the man who laid her in the grass, there was a black wolf over her, pinning her to the ground with his front paws. The head and face were the shape of a wolf, but the torso tapered to the shape of an extremely hairy man with a long, bushy tail rising from the buttocks.

Katherine screamed. The wolf raised its head and howled. Katherine was sure she heard laughter in the howl. She screamed until she lost consciousness.

Katherine

Katherine awoke in her own bed. Her head pounded, but that pain was a tickle compared to the raw ache she felt between her legs. Her bedroom was filled with the gray light of dawn and she wondered if the events of the night before had been a horrible dream brought on by a severe menstrual cycle. Then she saw that her window was still open and realized she was naked under the blanket. A muddy print, like that of a huge wolf, was visible on the windowsill. Katherine buried her face in the pillow, but there was no time to cry.

"Katherine? Are you awake?"

She took a deep breath and lifted her face from the pillow. "Yes, Mama."

"Your father is already in the barn and waiting for you to help him."

"Okay, Mama. I'll be right there."

Getting out of bed hurt. Most of the pain centered in her crotch, which she noticed had been cleaned of the blood she knew had been there. Her head throbbed now that she was on her feet and her muscles cried out in memory of the strenuous dancing around the fire.

What do I do? Do I tell Mama what happened?

She couldn't do that. Thomas hadn't raped her. She'd wanted him to do what he did. *It was the drink. He did something to the drink so that I wouldn't fight him.* She knew she couldn't prove that. *The wolf? Was he a wolf?* That was crazy. *Just another effect of the drink.* Katherine took the few shuffling steps to her closet and took down one of the two dresses hanging inside. The only other dress was the one she wore to church on Sundays. She dressed and slipped out the back door before her mother saw her. She winced as she walked to the milking barn, and she was glad when she had a cow in a station and was able to sit on the hard wooden stool.

"Are you feeling all right?" John asked.

"Uh-huh." Katherine pulled teats and shot milk into the bucket.

"Are you sure? It's not like you to oversleep. And you acted like you were hurting."

"It's just ... just a woman thing, Daddy."

"Oh." She knew he'd say no more about it; such subjects embarrassed him.

They finished milking and went to the house for breakfast. "Changing dresses in the middle of the week?" Katherine's mother asked.

"The other one had mud on it. From the creek," Katherine said.

"Well, you can go back to the creek and do some washing today, then."

"Yes, Mama."

"Katherine isn't feeling well," John said.

"Oh? What's wrong?"

"The curse of Eve."

"I can give you some powder for the pain." Mary patted Katherine on the shoulder and went to get the coffee pot from the stove.

Toward late morning, as Katherine was sweeping the front porch and wondering how she would explain the loss of her dress, she heard a wagon rattling quickly up the road and heard her father's voice shouting at the horses. She stopped sweeping and watched the cloud of dust on the road approach the entrance to their farm. As the lathered team of horses came swinging through the gate, pulling the wagon behind them with Katherine's father perched on the seat, Mary came out of the house to stand beside Katherine.

"Land sakes. There must be something dreadful

wrong to make him drive like that," Mary said.

"Whoa!" John reined the horses to a stop in front of the house and jumped to the ground. He rushed onto the porch and grabbed Katherine by the arms. His eyes were wide and sweat ran from under his hat as he stared intently at his daughter and tried to gather enough wind to speak. "Have you seen Elise? Elise Stone? She's missing."

"Missing?" Mary gasped, raising both hands to her mouth and turning her own eyes to her daughter's face.

"Missing?" Katherine asked, unable to say anything else, feeling like a trapped mouse under the scrutiny of her parents. She looked them both in the face, but couldn't hold the gaze. She began to cry.

"Katherine. Katherine, have you seen her recently?"

Katherine shook her head, telling her father the first lie she'd told since he switched her when she was five years old. He released her and went into the house. For a moment, Katherine thought he'd gone to find another switch. He came out of the house with a shotgun.

"What are you doing?" Katherine's mother asked.

"We're going out to the McGrath place. A lot of us men are going out there. We know the Stone girl had been sneaking away to see Luther."

"H–how do you know that?" Katherine asked.

"Do you know something about that?" John demanded. Katherine dropped her chin again and shook her head.

"Doc Yates told us. He said he's seen them together on the roads outside of town." Katherine's father jumped off the porch, climbed onto the wagon and had the horses running again before they reached the gate.

Katherine's mother wouldn't let her out of the house the rest of the day. The women remained inside, cleaning, sewing and preparing an evening meal they both knew probably would be stone cold before John returned home. At one point, Katherine took down the family Bible and sat in a patch of sunlight coming through the front window to read, but it seemed no matter what page she turned to she found reference to fornication, so she simply sat with the book open in her lap as the patch of sunlight moved across the room, dulled and finally faded away.

At about 10 p.m., long after the cows should have been milked, Katherine heard her father coming up the road in the wagon. She went to the front door, but her mother wouldn't let her open it. Outside, she heard the cows, gathered at the barn, calling for relief. Mary peeked from the curtains of a window, then said, "He's alone. We can go." She opened the door and Katherine followed her onto the porch.

John stopped the team in front of the house, but it was several moments before he looked at his women. Katherine and Mary waiting impatiently. Finally, he turned his face to them; it was haggard and very pale. His eyes seemed vacant and ... and scared.

"What happened?" Mary asked.

"Nothing. Nothing happened. They were gone. We found Elise. She's with Doc Yates now."

"What's wrong with her?" Katherine asked.

"She's bleeding inside."

"Oh, heavens," Katherine's mother said.

"Katherine, we need to milk the cows. I'll tend to the team while you get started."

"Is it safe?" Mary asked. It was another long moment before her husband answered.

"Damned if I know. But it's got to be done."

Hesitantly, Katherine left the porch and hurried to the milk barn. Her muscles still ached from the activity of the night before, but she did her best to walk normally. She was seated at her third cow when her father came in. She waited until he had a cow in place and was seated before speaking.

"What's wrong with Elise?"

"It's a woman thing," John answered. "She ... We think she was pregnant."

"*Was* pregnant?" Katherine was glad her father couldn't see her.

"Likely she's bleeding because she lost McGrath's bastard child. What would possess a nice girl like that, from damn fine parents, to take up with that clan? Did she ever say anything to you?"

"I don't know," Katherine said. "I don't know why she'd do it. Maybe they tricked her somehow."

"For the sake of her folks, I hope so."

"Did you ..." Katherine paused. "Did you find the men? Luther?" There was a long silence and Katherine was beginning to think her father wasn't going to answer.

"We agreed we'd never speak of it," he said at last. "But I feel like I should tell you. You and your mama. You should know." He paused again.

"What is it, Daddy?"

"They were there," he said. "We saw some of them in the cabin as we rode up. I don't know how many. We couldn't tell. But we saw Luther McGrath, big as day, step up to the window and look out as we were coming up. He closed the shutter of the window, stuck a rifle through a slat and shot Jess Parker. Killed him dead. Shot him in the head from fifty yards away. More of them started shooting at us, so we pulled back to the trees, all of us shooting back at the cabin."

Katherine finished the cow she was milking and sent her out the door and brought in another, pushing the beast's head toward the grain and closing the slats around her neck. As she finished getting the cow ready, John finished milking the cow he had and brought in another one.

"This went on for a few hours, them shooting at us and us shooting back at the house," he said when he resumed his stool. "And then, just about as the sun was starting to go down, Bart Schmidt starting yelling. He was behind a big oak tree kind of at the end of our line, so nobody could see him, really. Me and David Smith were the closest. I looked over and all I could see was Bart's legs, like he was lying on the ground and kicking.

"And then ..." he paused. "And then this monster wolf stepped away from the oak. Its whole head was covered in blood. It was dripping from its mouth. Bart wasn't moving no more. That wolf just looked at David and me, then real slow walked into the trees. Then I heard a man laughing, right in the area where the wolf had disappeared."

"I don't understand," Katherine said, although she understood much better than she wanted to.

"I don't understand it, either. But it got worse. That wasn't the only wolf. There was more, maybe a half-dozen. Soon they was in the trees behind us. We could see them back there, sitting and watching us. We ... we didn't know what to do because they were shooting at us from the cabin and these wolves were blocking us from behind."

"Daddy—" Katherine stopped, unsure what she had been about to say. "What did you do?"

"We talked, no, we argued for a bit about which was worse, the guns or the wolves. Then the wolves started moving closer. David took a shot at one of them but missed. We didn't have a lot of ammunition left by this time. We hadn't thought through what we were doing, I guess. We didn't expect a standoff. We sure didn't expect to be surrounded.

"The wolves rushed us then. Katherine, we broke and ran like rabbits. It shames me to say it, but we did. Most of us ended up running toward the cabin, using the bullets we had left to keep shooting ahead of us. I don't know about anyone else, but I was thinking of climbing on the roof to get away from the wolves.

"When we were just about twenty feet from the house, the door bust open and six more wolves come running out at us. They were big wolves. Vicious-looking wolves. They spilled out of the house and came at us. They coulda killed us. They coulda killed all of us. But they didn't. They just ran us around for a while, like dogs with sheep. The other wolves came down out of the trees and joined them, so there were about twelve of them, running twenty men around the yard of that cabin until we were about to fall down from being too tired.

"Then they herded us toward the cabin and chased us inside. That's where we found Elise. She was laying in a bed against the wall. She looked like she was already dead. Her face was pale and we couldn't get her to wake up at first. David's the one that took the blanket off her and saw that she was bleeding."

They both changed out their cows again. Katherine had finished hers first, but had sat transfixed until John was done and ready to get another cow. Once they were seated, she asked, "Is Elise going to be all right?"

"I don't know. I just don't know."

"How'd you get her out of the cabin and up to Dr. Yates?"

"The wolves left. I went and looked out one of the shutters and the yard was empty. I opened the shutter and leaned out to look, and sure enough, they were all gone. We didn't know if they'd come back or what, but we knew we had to do something about that girl. So, we wrapped her up in blankets, picked up what guns we could find bullets for, and a couple of men carried her while the rest of us walked around them, ready to shoot any wolves or McGraths we could find."

"Did you shoot anyone?"

"We didn't see anyone. No people. No wolves. Nothing. We carried Elise back to the trees and gathered up the horses that hadn't run off. We put Elise in my wagon and took her to Doc Yates's office. Wayne Charles rode ahead and got the doc out of his house so he could meet us there. Someone else went and got Elise's mama so she could be there with her girl. I stayed for a while because I knew you'd want to know how she's doing, but I couldn't find out anything. Doc Yates never came out of the office. I knew your mama would be worried, so I came on home."

"There were people in the cabin when you got there, but only wolves came out?" Katherine asked.

"That's how it was."

"Are they really devils? The McGraths."

"Sure looks that way. Wouldn't nobody believe it if they hadn't seen it, I know. But I saw it."

"I believe you, Daddy."

"You're a good girl, Katherine. I know you'd never get mixed up with trash like that."

"No, Daddy."

They finished the milking in silence, then went into the house to eat a cold supper. Katherine listened as her father retold his story. She watched him as he told it, noting how confused he looked, how he struggled to find words to relate the incredible events he'd witnessed.

"If anybody else told me that story, I'd say he was a liar or had been in the corn whiskey," Katherine's mother said when it was done. "What does it mean?"

"Daddy said they're devils," Katherine offered.

"They're not right," John agreed.

"Mama, what do you think is wrong with Elise?"

"From the sound of it, I'd say she was pregnant and had a miscarriage."

"You mean ..."

"The baby's dead," Mary said. "It can kill the

mother, too, if they can't stop the bleeding."

"Can Dr. Yates save her?"

"I don't know, child. You should go on to bed."

"I'm not really a child any more, Mama."

"What? What do you mean?"

"Nothing," Katherine said, poking at a bit of gravy on her plate. "I'm eighteen now."

"Oh, I know. You're still my child, though. No matter how old you are."

"Good night, Mama. Good night, Daddy."

Dr. Yates

Dr. Yates stood over the body of Elise Stone, rubbing his chin thoughtfully. In a tin pan between her bare legs lay two globs, still covered in blood, but recognizable as something that resembled stillborn puppies with tiny human arms. They had been dead when he removed them from the girl and dropped them into the pan.

The girl had not been dead then. She hadn't died until several hours later, as the doctor stood over her, soaking up the blood from his operation with a towel. There was a chance he could have saved her, but he refused to try.

"Why would I save you?" he asked the corpse. "So you could go back and try again to breed with them? You're better off dead. The world is better off that you're dead."

Dr. Yates continued to study the naked body before him. *How many doctors have had the opportunity to fully examine the body of a woman who has copulated with werewolves?*

The doctor wiped his hands and opened his office door. The parents of the girl had gone home for a while, thinking she was still alive but sleeping. Dr. Yates stepped onto his sidewalk and found a young boy loitering nearby. He tossed the youth a nickel and told him to fetch the schoolteacher.

"Tell him to wear work clothes," Dr. Yates said. "I have some things I need his help moving."

Katherine

"Dr. Yates and Fred O'Neal were put in jail today for Elise's death," John Cross announced to his family over dinner in late August. It was more than a week since Elise's decomposing body had been taken from the doctor's home and laid to rest in the Konawa City Cemetery.

"What did the schoolteacher have to do with it?" Mary asked.

"Seems he helped the doctor carry the body from his office to his house," John said. "And then ... he helped work on the body."

"They're monsters," Katherine said. "How could they cut her up like that?"

"Well, they're not in jail for what they did after she died," John said. "The county attorney and them other fellas dug her up yesterday and looked at the body. She died because Doc Yates took her baby out of her. He still won't say what he did with it."

"Excuse me." Katherine got up and left the table. She hurried to her room and closed the door, a hand held to her stomach and cold sweat on her forehead. She sat on her bed and concentrated very hard on not vomiting. She'd felt sick for a week now. Her mother attributed the morning vomiting to worry over Elise's death.

In the other room, Katherine could hear her mother complaining that the doctor was in jail when the person who should be locked up was Luther McGrath and all his family.

"Nobody can find them," John said.

It was true, Katherine knew. No McGrath had been seen since the day the men went to their cabin. However, everybody in the area was losing livestock to wolves and was afraid to venture outside after dark. The mournful sound of howling wolves had become a part of every evening.

Bile bubbled into Katherine's throat. She gulped, choked and managed to swallow it back down.

"Poor Elise," she murmured. "Please God, forgive her. Forgive me, too."

Dr. Yates had explained that Elise died of a congestive chill. He said he took the body to his house for study, to try to find a way to prevent the same affliction from happening to others. Katherine had heard stories that the doctor cut Elise into pieces. Some said it was to keep her from coming back from the dead.

Katherine sat for a while longer, her hands still on her belly. Today should have been the fourth day of her menstrual cycle, but it had not come. For the past two years, her cycle had been as regular as clockwork. She knew it would not be long before her mother connected the morning sickness and the lack of bloody rags indicating her cycle was in progress.

* * *

The next day, as Katherine was gathering eggs from the henhouse, she heard a commotion in the yard. She stepped out of the henhouse, glad to breathe air not filled with the smell of feathers and dung, and looked around. Most of the chickens and geese had run toward the house and were milling around the back porch, but had quieted. Katherine looked back at the dusting of uneaten grain she'd given the hens before going into the house after their eggs. She saw the print of a man's foot among the kernels.

"Over here," someone hissed.

Katherine looked up and found Thomas McGrath

standing at the corner of the barn, hidden from view of the house. He beckoned her closer. Katherine looked toward the house, wishing her mother would come out and call her so she wouldn't have to make the decision, but nothing happened. Hesitantly, she left the shadow of the henhouse and walked to the barn. Thomas stepped back so she could join him behind the building, where no one could see them.

"How are you?" he asked.

"You killed Elise," Katherine accused.

"No. No, it wasn't like that at all," he said. "She was losing the baby. We tried to help her. We were going to get a doctor when those men charged our house shooting at us."

"What about ..." Katherine stopped, unsure if she could say it. "What about the wolves?"

"What wolves?"

"My father said he saw people in the house, but only wolves came out. And there were wolves chasing the men out of the trees."

"Those weren't wolves. Those were just our dogs."

"No. I don't believe that."

"What are you saying? You believe I'm a werewolf. That we're all werewolves?"

"I know ... I know what you became that night," Katherine said, her voice barely a whisper. She looked around to make sure no one could hear them. "You were a wolf when you were on top of me. I saw it."

"You were drunk," Thomas said.

"Your cousin put something in that drink. I know that. But I know what I saw that night. And now ..."

"Now? Now what?" he said, seeming to perk up. He had been leaning against the wall and now pushed himself away, his dark eyes piercing her as if he would look inside her flesh.

"Nothing."

"Are you with child?"

"You should go. Just leave."

"Katherine, are you pregnant?"

She couldn't say it. Slowly, looking at the ground, she nodded her head once.

"Do you know what this means?" he asked, taking her by the arms.

"I won't marry you," she said. "I don't want to marry you. You and your family scare me."

"You are right, Katherine. You knew that. We are werewolves. We have been for hundreds of years. We live a very long time."

She looked up at him, saw his face full of excitement and knew that hers must show her doubt.

"I did become a wolf that night when we mated," he said. "It was a ritual dance we were doing. A fertility dance. It worked." He released her arms and put a hand on her stomach. She slapped it away and took a step back.

"Don't touch me," she said. "Daddy was right. You are a bunch of devils. All of you."

He laughed at her. "Devils? Why? Because we can do more than ordinary people can? Because we can change shape and become wolves? We're not devils. We're just not sheep."

"Is that what the rest of the world is to you? Just sheep?"

"A lot of people, yes. But you ... not you. Not now."

"Why?"

"You don't understand. No woman has ever given birth to a werewolf baby. That's what the ritual was for. We did the same for Elise."

"And she's dead because of it," Katherine said.

"Yes, she's dead."

"Why do you think I could live through it?"

"I don't know that you can. But if you do ... if you

do, you would be the one we have waited for. We've waited for centuries to find the Mother of the Pack."

"I don't want that. I don't want this," Katherine said, placing a hand over her womb.

"Luther was right," Thomas said. "He said these plains of the New World were fertile ground, but we thought he meant for game and grains. We didn't believe him when he said we would find the Mother here."

"I am not the Mother," Katherine said. "I'm just ... I'm just a girl you made sick with your drink so you could violate me. Please leave me alone. Just ... just leave."

"I'll go," he said. "I have to tell Luther. You know where our cabin is. When no one else will have you, come to us. We will be your new family when your own no longer wants you."

Katherine waited until he was gone, until he was out of sight of her tear-filled eyes before she sank to her knees behind the barn and cried harder than she'd ever cried before.

Katherine

"I've listened to you vomiting every morning for over a week, Katherine. I think it's time you told me about it."

Katherine sat at the kitchen table, nervously picking at a splinter in the wooden surface. She'd barely been able to help her father with the morning milking because she'd been so sick. The smell of sausage still hung in the air of the house, threatening to gag her at any moment. She stole a glance at her mother, standing at the end of the table, her arms crossed in front of her, waiting.

"We have to talk about it," Mary said, coming around the table to sit across from Katherine. She reached across the table and took her daughter's hand in her own. The grasp was soft and warm. Katherine began crying immediately.

"I–I'm ... I'm pregnant, Mama," she said between sobs. "Da–Daddy ... Daddy's going to—kill me."

"Hush, child," Mary soothed. "Nobody's going to kill you."

"It's—it's worse," Katherine said. "I—it's—was—Thomas—Thomas McGrath."

"McGrath?" Mary momentarily raised her hand from Katherine's, then dropped it back and gave her daughter's hand a gentle, hopeless squeeze. "Oh Katherine. Why? Why? Of all the boys? Of all the men it could have been. Why a McGrath?"

"I don't know, Mama," Katherine said, finally able to control her voice somewhat. "I went to find Elise, to bring her home. Thomas said maybe if I confronted her in front of Luther she'd see she was wrong and come home. That's when she told me she was pregnant. And

... and they gave me something to drink. It had something in it, something that made me all woozy. And then ... and then ... it happened."

"Oh Katherine. Oh my child," Mary said, tears coming to her own eyes.

"Mama?"

"What is it, baby?"

"He ... Thomas ... he turned into a wolf while he was on top of me."

Katherine saw the blood drain out of her mother's face and felt sure the temperature of the hand holding hers became colder in that instant.

"Katherine Ann Cross, you tell me that isn't so. You tell me you're making that up."

"No, Mama. I saw it. I opened my eyes, and I saw it. He was a man when he put his thing inside me. I closed my eyes because it hurt so bad and when I opened them he was ... he wasn't a man anymore."

Mary let go of Katherine's hand and stood up, she turned her back to Katherine, stood for a moment, then walked across the room to stand before the wall. She rested her head in her hands.

"Daddy's going to kill me, ain't he?"

"No, child. No," Mary said without looking back. "This will hurt him. It'll hurt him bad."

"I'm sorry, Mama."

Silence.

"I suppose you should go ahead and feed the birds," Mary said. "Gather the eggs."

"Mama?"

Silence.

"Thomas was here the other day. He was hiding out by the barn. I told him I'm pregnant. He said I could come to him, to his kin, when nobody else wanted me around."

Silence.

"I could go there. I could go away."

Mary turned around to face her daughter. Katherine saw her weathered face was wet with tears, her eyes red and shining with moisture. Her mouth quivered for a moment before she was able to speak. "You're not going anywhere, Katherine Ann Cross. You made a mistake, but we're your folks and we're going to love you no matter what."

"Mama." Katherine left the table as Mary rushed toward her and the two women met in the middle of the room and clung to one another for a long while. Finally, they separated, wiped at their faces and sniffled a few times. "I'll go feed the chicken and geese," Katherine said. She started for the door, then stopped. "Are we going to tell Daddy tonight?"

"I think we better."

Katherine nodded and went outside to do her chores.

* * *

Her father's reaction was not that different from her mother's. Katherine and Mary served the evening meal, putting all John's favorite dishes on the table, and sat quietly while they ate and listened attentively to his account of what had happened in town that day. When the meal was over, John leaned back, patted his stomach and commented on what a great meal it had been. He started to rise from his seat.

"John, there's something we need to talk about," Mary said.

"What's that?"

"Katherine is going to have a baby."

Katherine watched her father's face settle like a sack with the grain running out a hole in the bottom. He went from a contented smile over a good meal to suddenly looking like an old man with the weight of the world pressing at his shoulders. He stared at his empty plate for a long time before saying, "I didn't even know you had a fella."

"She was tricked," Mary said. "She went to help Elise and those McGraths tricked her."

"McGraths?" Now his head came up and a new light burned in his eyes. "A McGrath did it?"

Katherine, pinned under her father's eyes, could only nod in response.

"By God," John said. "By God ... which one?"

"T–Thomas."

John nodded slowly. "Nobody's seen any of them McGraths since ... since that day we went looking for Elise."

"I saw Thomas a couple of days ago, out by the barn," Katherine said.

"What? Here? On *my* land?"

"Yes, Daddy. He told me I could come stay with them; live with his family, if nobody else wanted me around."

"You'll not ever speak to another McGrath. Do you understand me, Katherine?"

"Yes, Daddy."

"We'll take care of this. We'll just keep this to ourselves. When the baby's born, we'll take it up to the convent and leave it with the nuns. They'll find a home for it. Until then, you just stay out of town."

Katherine started to protest, then stopped, unsure what she wanted to say. She didn't want to be pregnant, but the thought of giving up her own baby didn't seem right, either. She remained quiet.

"I think that's for the best," Mary said. "Don't you, Katherine? Don't you think your father is being very kind about this?"

Katherine nodded. "Yes, Mama," she said. Under the table, she slid a protective hand over her stomach.

Bernadette

Word got out, as it usually does in a small town.

Bernadette Sawyer and her 20-year-old daughter Mavis hosted tea every Wednesday afternoon. Bernadette could hardly wait until Mavis had served tea to their three guests—Lola Peters and her daughter Lindsey, and spinster Ruby Goshen—before gushing with the talk of the town.

"Did you hear about the Cross girl? Katherine?" she asked, leaning forward as she broke off a piece of cookie. She slipped the morsel into her mouth, then smoothed her pleated skirt as the other women nodded knowingly.

"Any girl who'd lay down for a McGrath is no account trash," Mavis said. The women murmured their agreement.

Fred

Fred O'Neal entered his classroom and placed his books on his desk. Usually the chatter of his students stopped when he entered the room, but today it continued. He looked up and most of the voiced died, but one conversation continued.

"She's pregnant," Betty Larson said. "I heard tell it was –"

"Betty?" O'Neal asked.

"Yes, Mr. O'Neal. I'm sorry."

O'Neal crossed his arms over his chest and clucked his tongue. "You know what they say about wagging tongues. Now, who is pregnant?"

"Haven't you heard? Katherine Cross. They say Thomas McGrath did it during some kind of satanic party."

The class erupted in shocked gasps and titters of amusement. O'Neal pulled the chair from his desk, the legs scraping loudly across the wood floor, and sat down heavily. *Oh God, not Katherine, too.*

Thomas

Thomas and Luther McGrath faced one another, their features lit by a dancing fire. Night birds called around them, but the men ignored the sounds, each focusing intently on the other.

"She's different. I know it. I feel it," Thomas argued.

"You don't know," Luther said. "You're too young. She won't be any different than the Stone girl or any of the others. She's going to die, Thomas. Forget about her."

"It was you who brought us here." Thomas leaned forward, the fire lighting his face more fully, making his eyes appear wide and almost mad. "You said the great plains of the New World is where we'd find the Mother. We're here. We've failed so far, yes, but Katherine is the one. She will live, and so will her child. My child. Our leader."

"No. We won't take her," Luther said. "It's too risky for us and I don't believe she has any better chance of living than any of the other girls."

"You're wrong, Luther. You're wrong."

"I am the leader here, Thomas. Unless you're ready to challenge the alpha male, you'll do what I say. Leave her. Forget about her."

Thomas looked away, then rose to his feet in one fluid motion and stomped away, leaving the older man behind.

John

Early October was still hot in the lumber mill. John Cross lifted his hat and wiped sweat from his brow with one hand while he fed rough lumber through a planer. The buzz of saws and roar of other machinery was very loud, but offered some privacy for his thoughts. Wood shavings flew through the air, coating John as he worked. As the last of his rough lumber went into the machine, Dale Edwards approached John and put a hand on his shoulder.

"I'm sorry to hear about your girl," Edwards shouted to be heard over the machinery.

"What's that?" John shouted back.

"Your girl. Katherine. I'm sorry to hear she let Thomas McGrath lay with her."

"Who told you that?" John yelled, knowing his voice gave away the truth of the statement.

"Nobody blames you or Mary, John. But you shouldn't have let her run around with that Stone girl. She was bad—"

He knew he shouldn't, but John couldn't stop the fist that flew up and punched Edwards in the face.

"You bastard!" Edwards yelled, blood running from his busted lip. He swung and caught John on the jaw. John staggered away a step, then came back at Edwards, grabbing the man by the shoulders to fling him to the floor. All around them, machinery was shut down and co-workers formed a circle to watch the fight.

John held Edwards down and punched him in the face and chest while blood from his own nose dripped onto the other man. Then he felt hands on his shoulders. They pulled him off Edwards, made him stand and held him away as other men helped Edwards to his feet. John looked around and saw that it was Roy Ford, the shop foreman, and Charles Keene, the mill owner, who was holding him. He looked away, saw Edwards standing across from him, the other man panting as hard as John was, then dropped his eyes to the sawdust-covered floor.

"John, come to my office," Keene commanded.

The arms holding him were released. Keene turned away and John followed him as the crowd of co-workers parted to let them through. In the office, Keene closed the door behind them, handed John a handkerchief for his nose, then poured him a cup of cool water before motioning John to a chair. Keene took up his tall leather chair behind the desk as John sat, the handkerchief held to his nose, the cup of water in his other hand.

"I imagine I know what that was about," Keene said. "The whole town is talking about your daughter."

John tried to think of a response, but could only sit silently for a long moment. Finally, he lowered his eyes and said quietly, "She's a good girl. They tricked her."

"I'm not judging you, or her, or anyone, John. You're a good man, a good worker. Always have been. I don't want to lose you, but I can't have you fighting in the shop."

John nodded. "Yes, sir. It won't happen again. I'm sorry."

"It's understandable," Keene said. "I'd have done the same thing if somebody spoke badly of my own daughter." Keene took a deep breath, then said, "You know, Dr. Yates can help you. Help Katherine. If she doesn't want the baby. I know he's helped other girls in similar circumstances."

John shook his head. "No, sir. We couldn't do that. It's not the baby's fault what happened. We plan to take it to the convent after it's born."

Keene nodded. "All right. If you change your mind—

if Katherine changes her mind—a tell Doc Yates I recommended you to him. Now, go on back to work."

"Yes, sir. Thank you." John left the chair and the office, closing the door behind him.

Kill the baby?

John shook his head, ignoring the looks from the other men in the mill as he returned to his station. *Kill the baby? It would be like this never happened.*

He took up another piece of raw lumber, studied it for a moment without really seeing it, then fed it through the planer.

Katherine

When John came home with a swollen nose and news that people in town had finally stopped giving him looks of pity and had begun asking outright about the condition of his daughter, Katherine knew it was because the other people who had been at the McGraths' that night had told at least the main part of what had happened.

Did they tell how Thomas turned into a wolf?

She doubted that. A few people had ventured out to the farm in hopes of seeing the girl everyone had always thought so sweet but who really was a whore with such low standards she'd lay down for a McGrath. Mary turned them all away in the yard, not even accepting the gifts that were brought as an excuse for the visits.

The humans weren't the only ones nosing around. Day and night, but especially at night, the trees around the Cross house were filled with the singing of wolves. The sound kept everyone on edge, wondering if the McGraths were going to rush the house to take Katherine away, to kill her parents, or just try to drive them insane with the incessant howling.

"Mama, why am I so big?" Katherine asked one day in early October.

"I wanted to ask you about that," Mary said, sitting down at the kitchen table with her daughter. Together, they snapped green beans to boil for the evening meal. "Tell me true, Katherine. Was that one time you told me about the only time you ever was with a man? You never did it before then?"

"No, Mama. Never."

"Then I reckon the only explanation can be that

you're carrying more than one baby," Mary said. "It's just been about two months since that night, but you look like you're five months along in your time."

"Do you think ... do you think I'm all right? Should I see a doctor?"

"I suppose you should. I'll have your father see about getting Doc Goodwin out here."

Dr. Goodwin refused to come, having heard rumors of Katherine's public copulation with several of the McGraths in some kind of witchcraft ritual. Two days later, John Cross brought home the only doctor in Konawa who would see his daughter. Mary opened the door to admit the two men.

"Dr. Yates, thank you for coming," Mary said. "Katherine isn't feeling well at all."

"What's wrong with her?" John asked.

"She's been laid up all day. Says she's having sharp pains in her belly."

"It's not uncommon," the doctor said. "Take me to her."

Mary led the doctor to Katherine's room, knocked and quickly opened the door. Katherine lie in her bed, her face drawn and pale. She turned her head and looked at the doctor as he entered her bedroom, her eyes widening at the sight of him.

"They say you killed Elise," Katherine said, her voice husky.

"Katherine," Mary snapped. "Dr. Yates was good enough to come see you. Besides, there was no truth to that. If there was, he wouldn't be out of jail." Mary turned to the doctor. "I'm sorry to have to mention that. It must have been hard for you to endure."

The doctor only grunted in response. "If you'll leave us alone, I'll examine her," he said. Mary and John withdrew, closing the door behind them. "I'm going to have to feel inside you," the doctor said. Without waiting for Katherine's response, he pulled away the covers of the bed. "Lift your knees," he ordered. Katherine did and he pushed her gown up to her waist, then stuck his hand inside her.

Katherine screamed as the hand dove into her, twisted this way and that, pushed here and there, and finally withdrew. The doctor pulled her gown back over her knees and carelessly draped a blanket over her.

"One of the McGraths did this?" he asked.

Katherine nodded. The doctor came to stand beside her head, looking down at her, his eyes cold, his face set. He held his right hand before him and Katherine could see blood on his fingers. "Is it true you lay down for all the McGrath men?"

"No," Katherine said, still hurting too much to acknowledge the accusation. She could feel blood oozing from her loins. "It was just ... it was Thomas."

"I saw you going out there that night. I knew no good would come of it."

"I went to get Elise."

"It was too late for her. Did Thomas McGrath take the shape of a wolf while you were with him?"

Katherine felt her blood freeze for just a moment. She slowly rolled her eyes up to meet the doctor's look. "You know?"

"I know a lot about the McGraths. And others. I know that if you live through this pregnancy, which I doubt, you'll become a werewolf, too. The thing, or things, you have inside you right now are of their blood, and that blood is contaminating you every day you are pregnant."

"I–I'll be ... like them?"

"Yes."

"Isn't there anything you can do to help me?"

"There is only one known cure," he said. "I'm going to go talk to your parents."

Katherine watched his back as he left the room. He didn't close her bedroom door all the way. She could hear him talking to her mother and father in the other room, but couldn't make out the words. It sounded as though Mary and John were arguing with the doctor, but the longer they talked, the less conviction they had in their voices. Finally, all three returned to Katherine's room.

"Doc Yates is going to take you back into town. To his office," John said. "He says he can only take care of you there. He has the equipment he needs there."

"No, Daddy. I don't want to go," Katherine said.

"Hush, child," Mary said. "It's going to be all right. Dr. Yates said he's dealt with this kind of problem lots of times."

"This kind of problem?" Katherine asked.

"He said the baby is pushing against some of your insides, your liver and lungs and such, and that's causing the pains. He'll watch over you for a few days and, if the pain doesn't stop, he'll have to move the baby," Mary said.

"Move the baby? How?"

"It's a special procedure," the doctor interrupted. "Now, if you folks don't mind, we should put her in the wagon and take her to my office."

John stepped forward and scooped his daughter from the bed. "Daddy, I don't want to go," Katherine said. "I ... I don't trust him."

"You'll be all right, Katherine," John said. "And nobody else would come. Be thankful there's a doctor to help you."

Katherine didn't speak again as John carried her to Dr. Yates's wagon and lay her in the back of the buckboard. She didn't respond as her parents promised to come visit her as soon as they could, assured her she would be fine, waved to her and finally were out of site as the doctor set his team of horses in motion. The doctor made no attempt to speak to her and Katherine did not speak to him during the ride into town.

"You can walk," he said when he stopped the wagon at the rear entrance to his office.

Painfully, Katherine stood up. She refused the doctor's hand in climbing down from the wagon and followed him into his office. He took her to a small room with a narrow bed and told her to sleep. "I'll be in off and on to check on you," he said, then closed the door on her.

The room was small and sparse. Other than the narrow bed, the only furnishings were a wooden chair, a small table and a washstand with a clay basin and pitcher. A white towel with brownish stains on it hung from the rack of the washstand. Katherine knew the stains were from blood. She wondered if it was Elise's blood.

The pains in her abdomen were sharp enough to keep her hunched over. She pulled back the covers of the bed and eased herself onto the hard mattress, pulling the covers over her waist. She lay quietly most of the time, though at times she cried out when a pain was particularly sharp. She dozed, and eventually woke up knowing she had a fever. She opened her eyes and needed a drink. Her mouth was sticky and filled with a bad taste.

"You can't do that to her."

Katherine remained still, her mouth open, unsure if she was awake or having a fever dream. She believed she saw Dr. Yates at the end of the bed arguing with the schoolteacher, Fred O'Neal.

"Suppose she gives birth to this thing?" Yates said. "Are we going to let her go? Are we going to let her walk out of here with the warrior leader they've been looking for?"

"All right," Fred said, shaking his head. "The baby, fine. I understand that. But why her? Why Katherine?"

"She's one of them now."

"Then after this time, she won't be able to breed again. To get pregnant."

"We don't know that," Yates said. "The change probably will destroy her womb, but it may not. We can't risk it. She—"

"Water," Katherine croaked, unable to endure any more. The men froze, the doctor with his hand in mid-gesture, the schoolteacher with his mouth open to speak. Both their heads swung around to look at Katherine. "Water," she repeated. "I'm so thirsty. I have a fever."

Dr. Yates nodded to Fred and the schoolteacher poured water from the wash pitcher into a tin cup. He handed it to Katherine and she drank; the water was warm and tasted dusty. She asked for more.

"Am I going to die?" she asked the doctor.

"Probably," he answered.

"You're going to kill me."

He stared at her without answering. Katherine turned her eyes to her former teacher.

"Please don't let him kill me," she said.

"Hush, Katherine. Everything's going to be fine," Fred answered. "Dr. Yates will do what's best."

"I hurt real bad. The pains just keep coming, like somebody's stabbing me with a long knife."

"It's your body changing," the doctor said. "You're becoming a wolf. A bitch wolf."

Katherine cried until she fell asleep again. In her dreams, the doctor and schoolteacher continued discussing her.

"I thought only silver could kill a werewolf," Fred said. "Silver or wolfsbane."

"She's not a werewolf yet. This will do it," Yates answered.

"It's cruel. You should at least do it quickly."

"I want to see this baby alive if possible," Yates said. "She has a single heartbeat coming from her womb. Just one. The Stone girl had two. The one before her had three. They ruptured and died early. They would have died without my help. This one, though, has only one heartbeat and she's carried the thing inside her for two months. This may be the one."

"Are you ..."

Katherine drifted deeper into sleep before Fred finished his next question. She dreamed of a deep, dark forest, of drums and dancing and pain from within her body. After the pain was a sense of fierce freedom. She ran on four legs, ran faster than she'd ever run on two legs. And she sang duets to the moon with Thomas McGrath.

She woke up screaming and found that her wrists and ankles were bound to the bed. Her clothes were gone. Dr. Yates stood at the foot of the bed, between her ankles, a bloody instrument in his hand. Fred O'Neal stood beside her, his face pale.

"She *is* the one," Yates said. "She *is* the Mother of the Pack." His eyes were directed to Katherine's lap, just as the schoolteacher's were. Katherine felt a warm burning there and looked down.

There was so much blood. Her lower torso and upper thighs were bathed in bright red blood that glistened in the light from the lanterns and candles placed around the room. From her naval to her crotch, Katherine saw that her flesh was split open and gaping like the drooling mouth of a happy lunatic.

"Look at it," the doctor said. He dangled a lantern over Katherine's crotch with one hand. With the other, the one holding the dripping scalpel, he reached for the slit in her belly. Katherine felt him reach into her and grip her flesh from the inside with the fingers and the outside with his thumb. The pain as he pulled the opening wider almost made her lose consciousness. As she looked again, she wished she had passed out.

Inside herself, shiny and wet in the light of the kerosene lantern, she saw her child. The baby was curled into a ball, its forearms and legs pulled tight against its body, its head pressed between the knees of the hind legs. It had the body of a tiny human infant, the hairless tail of an unborn wolf cub, hind legs like a wolf but with the smallest of human feet. The arms also were wolfish, but one had a human hand. Blood pumped from Katherine's veins, baptizing the child in the blood of its mother.

"Hold the light," Dr. Yates said. Fred reached over and took the lantern. His shaking hand caused shadows to dance within the wound. Katherine wanted to look away, but couldn't.

Outside, in the night, several wolves howled.

"You're too late," the doctor answered the beasts. With one hand, he snatched the deformed child from the womb. He held it over Katherine, the umbilical cord connecting the rat-size body to her own. Blood dripped from the baby and seemed to hang in the air as if refusing to fall back into the open womb. Dr. Yates whisked the scalpel across the infant's throat and its wolfish head popped off like a cork and fell onto Katherine's bare chest.

"Uhhhh–uhhhhhhhhhh-uhhhhhhhhhhhhh." Katherine wanted to scream, but couldn't. She was too weak, too scared. The closed eyes of the severed head seemed to stare at her. Her head fell back onto the pillow.

"Now what?" Fred asked.

"I'm done with the bitch," Dr. Yates said.

"She's bleeding. She'll bleed to death."

"If it worries you, do something about it."

Katherine was aware of the doctor leaving the room.

"He killed me," she whispered. Bubbles of blood formed with her saliva burst as she spoke, showering her face in sticky crimson. "You said he wouldn't."

Fred O'Neal seemed to loom over her suddenly. "I'm sorry, Katherine," he said. "It's for the best. They can never be allowed to have a naturally born child."

"I'm dying," she said.

"This is all I can do for you, Katherine. Forgive me."

Fred O'Neal pulled the pillow from under Katherine's head and pressed it over her face. She didn't struggle. Instead, she closed her eyes and welcomed the darkness.

Thomas

School had let out about an hour ago. Thomas McGrath had waited until the last students had straggled away from the small schoolhouse at the end of the street before he crossed from one hiding place to another in the space between the school and a mercantile. It was an overcast, cold day that threatened rain at any moment.

He waited patiently, and soon the teacher he wanted exited the building. Thomas stepped from the alley, grabbed Fred O'Neal by the throat with one hand and covered the man's mouth with the other as he dragged him into the shadows between the buildings. He threw O'Neal against the brick wall of the school and stepped close so that his face was only inches from the teacher's.

"Did you kill her, then?" Thomas asked.

"Wha-? Who?" His eyes widened as he realized who he was facing. "Thomas McGrath."

"Aye. In the flesh. The human flesh, for the moment, my friend. Tell me true and I might let you live. Did you kill Katherine Cross?" Thomas asked.

O'Neal shook his head slowly. "No. It wasn't me. It was Yates. The doctor did it."

"You were there. I know you were," Thomas said.

O'Neal nodded. "I killed her. I killed her. But she was already dying. Yates cut her open. He took ... he took a—a thing out of her. She lost a lot of blood. She was dying. I just made it easier for her. I didn't want to. I liked her."

Thomas relaxed just a little. He backed away, but remained close enough to prevent any chance of O'Neal escaping. "There was a baby, then? You could tell it was a baby?"

"Y-yes. It—it wasn't normal. It was ... part wolf."

"Aye. It was my child," Thomas said quietly.

O'Neal looked hopefully past Thomas toward the opening of the alley. "Are you going to kill me?"

"Should I?"

O'Neal shook his head vigorously. "I pray you don't."

"I think I won't, though I likely should."

The relief that washed over O'Neal was visible and seemed to embolden the man. "Are you really what Yates says? A werewolf?" he asked.

Thomas glared at the man, then, without speaking, he called the wolf, shifting to his in-between shape that was neither wolf nor human. He lunged forward, growling, and bit the schoolteacher's shoulder. O'Neal screamed. Thomas released him and changed back to his human shape while O'Neal clutched his bleeding shoulder.

"My cousin, Luther, won't tolerate a stray in his territory," Thomas said. "Now that you're like us, you should get as far away as possible. Before he finds out you're one of us. Before he comes to kill you."

O'Neal looked at the blood seeping around his fingers, then back to his attacker. Thomas smiled, showing the blood on his teeth. O'Neal ran from the alley. Thomas went the other way, exiting behind the buildings.

* * *

The rain had come just as the graveside funeral started. From his hiding place within the cedar trees at the north border of the cemetery, Thomas watched the mourners break apart and drift away, all except John and Mary Cross. The bereaved mother stood over the fresh grave and cried uncontrollably as her husband tried to comfort her.

"Come on, Mary. We should go home now," John said.

Mary shook her head savagely. "Were we bad, John? Are we responsible for this? Is it our fault?"

John signed. "Maybe. Maybe not. There's nothing to be done for it. She's with God now. We should go home."

"What about the McGraths?" Mary asked.

"Sheriff says he can't do anything about them. With Katherine ... she can't accuse them of anything now. She can't accuse anyone."

Thomas saw John's eyes fix on Yates as the doctor moved toward the gate of the cemetery.

"I'm going to miss her so much, John. I do miss her already," Mary said.

John put his arm around his wife's waist. They were both soaked by the rain. "I know you are," he said. "We both are. Let's go home." They turned and made their way slowly toward the cemetery gates.

Thomas watched them go, waiting until he could be alone with the grave. He heard a step behind him and caught Luther's scent a moment before the man put a familiar hand on Thomas's shoulder.

"Our time here is over," Luther said quietly. "We're moving on."

"Where?" Thomas asked without looking at his cousin.

"The Dakotas. I still believe these fertile plains will produce the Mother, but it's no longer safe for us here. We'll go north."

"Not me. I have business here," Thomas said, his gaze resting on Yates as the doctor paused at his buggy to return a greeting from another mourner.

"You see the new bulge in the doctor's coat?" Luther asked. "He carries a gun now. I do not doubt that his revolver is loaded with silver bullets. Any advantage you might have had was lost when you let the schoolteacher live."

Thomas finally looked to Luther for a moment, then returned his attention to John and Mary as they made their way out of the cemetery. "You know about that already?"

Luther chuckled softly. "Yes. Of course. I let him go. For now. Let him live with what he fears so much for a while. We can deal with him later."

"I'm tired of it, Luther. The killing. The raping. Looking for the Mother. All of it."

"Of being a werewolf?"

"No. Not that," Thomas said.

"What will you do?"

"I will dog his steps. He will spend every moment he has left knowing that I am nearby, wondering when I will come to avenge Katherine."

"The girl meant so much to you?" Luther asked.

Thomas nodded. "Yes. Yes, she did. Even before I knew she was the one."

"The schoolteacher likely didn't know what he was talking about. He was afraid and probably telling you what he believed you wanted to hear."

"He was telling me the truth."

"I cannot make you come with us, Thomas, though I wish you would."

Thomas looked to Luther again and smiled a genuine smile. He held out his hand and Luther took it firmly in his own. "We'll meet again, cousin," Thomas promised.

Luther nodded. "Be well," he said. He withdrew his hand and walked away.

Thomas watched John and Mary leave the cemetery. He waited several more moments before leaving his hiding place and approaching Katherine's grave. The smell of the freshly turned earth was very strong. He knelt beside the marker and touched her name, then

moved his hand to the bottom of the stone and traced his fingers over the epitaph, *Murdered by human wolves.*
"Not werewolves," Thomas murmured.

Epilogue

"Come on, Mary," John urged. All the other people had left the cemetery. The rain was still coming down in a steady drizzle. He stood behind his wife, watching her and looking around to see if anybody or any*thing* was watching them. "We should go on home now."

"Were we bad, John?" Mary asked. "Was this our fault?"

"Maybe. Maybe not. There's nothing to be done for it now."

"Will they keep that horrible doctor in jail this time, do you think?"

"I can't say."

"And what about the McGraths?"

John sighed. "Sheriff says he can't do anything about them. With Katherine ... she can't accuse them of anything now."

The rain had soaked his best suit and made it cling to his body. John felt a chill coming on. Behind him, tied to a post outside the stone fence surrounding the cemetery, his horses snorted and stomped impatiently. October wind pushed across the cemetery from the west, making the raindrops sting John's neck.

"I'm going to miss her so much, John" Mary said and softly wept at the loss of her only child. "I do miss her already,"

"I know you are. We both are," John said.

John watched as Mary traced the final lines on Katherine's grave with a shaky finger. Then she stood, straightened her skirt and quickly wiped both eyes. He put his arm around her and led her out of the cemetery, helped her onto the wagon, and they went home.

KATHERINE
Dau. of
J.T. & M.K.
CROSS
Mar. 18, 1899
Oct. 10, 1917
Murdered by human
wolves

Steven E. Wedel

On the Trail of Werewolves: An Interview with Mary Franklin, Paranormal Investigator

If you'd asked her about it five years ago, Mary Franklin said she would have told you she didn't believe in werewolves. Ask her today and her answer is somewhat different.

"I would have to say I don't know," she said.

The reason for her wavering disbelief centers on a tombstone in the Violet/Konawa Cemetery just west of the town of Konawa in central Oklahoma. The tombstone belongs to Katherine Cross, an 18-year-old girl born March 13, 1899, and died on October 10, 1917. The epitaph carved on her grave marker says Cross was "Murdered by human wolves."

Mary Franklin is a native of eastern Oklahoma who has been doing paranormal research for over a decade. She isn't ready to say that Cross was indeed killed by werewolves. However, she is sure Cross did not die a natural death, that she was not the only young person in the Konawa area to suffer a violent death within a period of a few years, and that some entities—some humans and some who may be something other than human—do not want the truth known.

City records for that time period are missing. There was a fire at Konawa's city hall and records were lost. But, the local library also is missing all relevant information from 1916 and 1917, Franklin said.

"Record keeping was poor or lost or stolen," Franklin said. "Or just hid away forever from the public. Konawa holds many dark secrets on these deaths."

According to one of Franklin's sources, an elderly woman living in Konawa at the time, there were 86 mysterious, violent deaths during those years. At least some of them can be attributed to Dr. A.H. Yates and Fred O'Neal, a Konawa schoolteacher.

An article posted online through USGENWEB by Linda Simpson, Indian Territory Archivist, says that Yates and O'Neal were arrested for performing a "criminal operation" on Cross. The arrest was announced in *The Seminole County News* newspaper on October 25, 1917. This was the second charge in two months for the men.

According to the newspaper article quoted by Simpson, Elise Stone was admitted to Yates's office on August 15 and remained there for four days. After four days, she was taken to Yates's home. She died; Yates attributed her death to a "congestive chill." Suspicious, some townspeople contacted County Attorney A.G. Nichols. With an order from M.L. Rascoe, justice of the peace, Nichols and the county physician exhumed the body of Stone and did an autopsy in the graveyard. It was determined she had died from a "criminal operation." The article by Simpson speculates that both Stone and Cross died during abortions, which where illegal and considered highly immoral at the time.

Simpson closes her article by stating, "The human wolves weren't werewolves or any other supernatural monster. They were a doctor and a schoolteacher."

Franklin said she has not found the grave or any further information about Stone. Nor can she confirm that 86 people were killed in Konawa at that time or that Yates and O'Neal were involved in that number of murders. "I know when you go through the cemetery list of people who died in this time there were a lot of young people who died and were buried in this area in a short time," she said.

"I believe neither Katherine Cross nor Elise Stone died of natural causes," Franklin said. "I know they were murdered."

Murdered by werewolves? Or by werewolf hunters?

Franklin said she first learned of Cross when a friend e-mailed her about the legend of a headstone in the Konawa cemetery that had the inscription, "Murdered by human wolves."

Franklin said, "In the legend, the story was told that the young girl had been murdered by unknown forces. I accepted the case and loaded up equipment for a hot and long journey to Konawa."

Deciding to spend a whole Saturday in the cemetery, Franklin said she and her crew set out on Friday evening. At about 8 p.m., after turning onto Highway 31 in Ada, Franklin said they saw something unusual.

"To our right was the largest silver-colored wolf I had ever seen in my life, no more than 10 feet from the road, staring at our car," she said. "It never moved, just stared at us."

That wasn't the end of the strange events. Upon finding the cemetery, Franklin said they saw a small shack in a corner of the graveyard. Thinking the cemetery had a caretaker who could show them where the headstone was the next morning, the crew retired for the night in an Ada motel. When they returned the next morning, there was no building in the cemetery.

Franklin said the local police had agreed to meet her in the cemetery at 7 a.m. that Saturday. She said the police claimed to have no knowledge of the cryptic headstone. Franklin and her crew spent the next several hours searching the small cemetery for the marker of Katherine Cross.

"After four hours of footwork, we were tired and hot. I was going to call the investigation off," she said. "Then, to my left, it sounded like an old railroad spike hit a headstone. It did. An old, worn railroad spike rested at my right foot. And there was Katherine Cross's headstone staring at me."

Franklin said events continued to get more mysterious as the investigation went on. During her first visit, she did 45 minutes of Electrical Voice Phenomena (EVP) recordings in which she would ask a question at Cross's grave while a tape recorder picked up sound in the area. The assertion by paranormal researchers is that the recorder can often capture ethereal voices not audible to the human ear until they are played back.

"I was shocked with what I got," Franklin said. "As I stood in the cemetery alone, listening to the questions I had asked her, she told me she was murdered by a Dr. Yates. Who he was, at this time I had no idea. But six months down the road I found out yes, her killer was the local doctor and his name was Dr. Yates."

Franklin described Cross's voice as very soft. Immediately after Cross revealed who her killer was, Franklin said another voice came across on the tape.

"The tape became distorted by what sounded like wind blowing with a high-pitched wailing. Then a guttural male voice broke in, saying, 'Get out! I won't tell you again, get out! I will kill you. I will come out of this grave and kill you.' This shook me very badly," Franklin said.

Franklin said at the time she had not intended to spend more than a day investigating Cross's grave, thinking the whole story was nothing but local legend. "How much did I know that Katherine Cross was about to change my life and way of thinking?" she said.

Yates, it turns out, is buried not far from Cross. Franklin said she ordinarily does not bother with Yates's grave, but on a whim once, she did a 30-minute EVP at the doctor's grave. "I asked him if he killed Katherine and if there were werewolves in Konawa," Franklin said. "I got a one-word answer that is very plain: 'Several'."

Franklin said she now believes that Yates and O'Neal probably killed some number of people out of suspicion the victims were werewolves.

Are there werewolves in Konawa?

Franklin stopped short of answering, but related more strange happenings she witnessed during her visits to the cemetery. In one instance, she said, she was in the cemetery, this time with her children who were helping her. She had her audio and video equipment set up, along with array meters used for picking up electro-magnetic fields.

"Suddenly we heard howling," she said. "It was coming from in the cemetery, but none of my meters had gone off." Franklin said she gathered her kids, equipment and left.

She took an audiotape of the event to an expert she knows and asked him what was making the sound. "He told me it was the biggest timber wolf he'd ever heard. And there were several of them," she said.

Soon after, she said she got an e-mail message from a man claiming to be a member of a clan of werewolves living in Konawa. Franklin said she was ready to dismiss the man as a crazy until he mentioned seeing her and her children in the cemetery, and how they'd fled when the howling began.

Sometime later, the same person e-mailed her again and asked her to meet with two men in the cemetery. "He said I could bring one camera, but no weapons and I had to come alone," she said. "That wasn't going to happen."

Franklin arrived at the cemetery with a video camera equipped with a good telephoto lens. Using the zoom of the camera, she said she found the two men, who appeared to be in their 80s, standing at the other side of the graveyard.

"When I first saw them, it looked like their eyes were glowing," she said. "But I just assumed it looked that way through the camera. But then they saw me, and they came sprinting toward me like teenagers. I turned around and started running back to my car, but I knew I'd never get there in time because those guys were running like sixteen-year-old boys. I thought, 'God, if I'm going to die, at least I'll have it on tape'."

At that moment, her cousin, who had arrived after her, appeared from the trees surrounding the cemetery and asked why she was running. Franklin stopped and pointed behind her. "But they were gone," she said.

Determined to find the truth
Despite the bizarre happenings, only some of which she says she has related here, Franklin is not giving up on finding out what really happened to Katherine Cross.

"The story goes that Katherine Cross died from a very bad abortion," Franklin said. "If so, then why was it necessary to shred her body up? I do know that this is one of the most covered-up stories I have yet to run across."

At one point, on about her seventh trip up to Konawa, Franklin said an elderly woman who knew she was researching Cross approached her. "She told me, 'Be very careful. There are creatures in these woods not known to man.' And she turned and left and never said another word."

The possible werewolf killings are not confined to just Konawa, though. Franklin said she also is looking into reports of murders attributed to human wolves and human dogs in the small towns of Thackerville and Stonewall. She said a cemetery near Stonewall once had 19 headstones that bore the epitaph "Murdered by werewolves." Those stones have since been destroyed or stolen, she said.

"I have stumbled onto something," Franklin said. "What, I don't know. I have a lot of hard hours of research poured into [Cross's] case. I have very little; there isn't a lot on her. She has become my life.

"The area holds many secrets but I will continue to go back until I find the answers."

Afterword

It's a small, small world. I wrote this book in 2003. In January of 2007 I became a high school English teacher in an independent Oklahoma City school district. In 2009 I had a student in class who, it turns out, is Katherine Cross's great-niece.

How can this be, you ask, since there is no mention in this story of Katherine having a brother or sister? I could claim artistic license, but the truth is it was sloppy journalism and a very, very tight deadline, followed by, well, I don't know. Laziness, probably. Remember, the book was first written to be a freebie and the idea for the story wasn't given to me until about a month before the original version of *Shara* was set to be released. I did some research, but I relied too much on one source for most of my information, and that source never mentioned that Katherine had any siblings.

I could have changed that for this edition, but I chose not to do so. We'll call it artistic license now. Katherine's family isn't at all pleased about this book's existence.

I'd just like to say that I didn't write this story to exploit the real-life tragedy of Katherine Cross. What was done to her was horrible and frightening and nearly unimaginable. Katherine has passed into legend in Oklahoma. Her grave—and that of Dr. Yates—are listed on many paranormal Web sites and she even has her own Wikipedia page. As with many writers, I simply asked that question, "What if …?" What if there really had been werewolves in Konawa in 1917? What if they weren't the worst monsters in the area at the time? This story is the result of those musings.

Steve can be found online at
www.stevenewedel.com

www.ingramcontent.com/pod-product-compliance
Lightning Source LLC
Chambersburg PA
CBHW020119180726
47992CB00019B/1026